A PLACE TO CALL HOME

Guy and Sarah Randle enjoy a good lifestyle in Germany with their daughters Briony and Ellie, but when Guy's employers close the company, they have to face many changes. They decide to return to England, although Briony insists on going to France with her boyfriend Fabien. Guy reluctantly agrees to move in with his parents and take over his ailing father's business, but there are many adjustments to make as three generations settle in together. They have to cope with an unexpected pregnancy, an adopted dog and dwindling finances, before they learn to compromise and arrive at a solution which suits them all!

A PLACE TO CALL HOME

A PLACE TO CALL HOME

by

Sue Moorcroft

Dales Large Print Books
Long Preston, North Yorkshire,
BD23 4ND, England.

British Library Cataloguing in Publication Data.

Moorcroft, Sue
    A place to call home.
    A catalogue record of this book is
    available from the British Library

    ISBN   978-1-84262-544-6 pbk

Published in Large Print 2007 by arrangement with
Sue Moorcroft, care of MBA Literary Agents

Dales Large Print is an imprint of Library Magna Books Ltd.

Printed and bound in Great Britain by
T.J. (International) Ltd., Cornwall, PL28 8RW

Chapter One

'Come in, lovely to see you!' Sarah Randle, smart and attractive in a new summer dress, beamed as she flung open the door to the first guests. 'We're eating outside, go through and join the others. Ellie's in charge of the cold drinks, I'm afraid Guy's been held up at work.'

'Nothing new there, honey,' her friend Virginia observed drily, stepping inside as her three children dashed off in the direction of the garden. 'Guess you'll just have to do the entertaining alone – and on your anniversary, too!' She dropped a peck on Sarah's cheek.

Sarah turned the unfamiliar weight of the thick silver bracelet which Guy had given her to mark their twenty-first wedding anniversary. 'Never mind, it's always lovely to see you all.'

As all their relatives were back home in England, friends were very important to the Randle family and Sarah loved to throw open the comfortable home so typical of this lovely part of Germany. Mikhlut, the pretty, friendly village in which they lived looked out from the side of a hill, giving them a view of neat farmlands and dark forests.

Two further cars disgorged their families outside the house, and she stepped out into the sunshine to greet them. 'Katrine! Paula and Stephen! Aren't we lucky with the weather? I couldn't resist taking the party outdoors.'

As Sarah ushered in the new arrivals a tall, blonde-streaked woman strolled into view, pushing a gaily chequered pram. 'I was wondering where you were, Marika,' Sarah hailed. Marika Rundschke lived only half-a-mile away and was Sarah's closest friend.

'Grüss Gott,' responded Marika, giving the traditional greeting. 'If I am late for your party it is the fault of baby Hannah. She will not hurry her meals.'

'Grüss Got! You're not late at all because you're about the most organised new mum I've ever known.' She hugged the younger woman and led her through to the garden. 'Where's Josef?'

Marika turned down her mouth. 'Work, my husband remains late, always.'

'Guy's been delayed, too. *GB Schwarz* are great employers, but they expect a lot for their money.' Their husbands worked together at the head office of a European haulage giant, an imposing, mirrored glass building on an industrial estate. The red-and-black livery of the huge *GB Schwarz* lorries could be seen on any road of any continental country.

Marika parked baby Hannah in the shade, and nodded towards a corner of the garden. 'I see we have the boyfriend of Briony?'

Sarah glanced over to where her eldest daughter, 18-year-old Briony, lounged in a grassy corner, her dark head close to that of the young man sprawling beside her. 'Yes, Fabien. His work experience here is almost up, he'll be going home to France, soon. Briony's going to be heartbroken.'

'But she goes to university in September?'

'They both do – but hers will be in England, his in France!' As they watched, Briony picked something from Fabien's shirt, and Fabien captured her hand to kiss her fingertips. Sarah smothered a sigh. It seemed no time since it was Briony lying in her pram, gazing up with Guy's dark eyes, as cute and helpless as Hannah was today.

'And you are to be heartbroken when Briony goes back to England,' Marika sympathised shrewdly.

Sarah pulled a face. 'I'm trying not to think about it.'

She shook off any threatening gloom, leaving Marika to join a group as she took up her hostess duties, joining her younger daughter Ellie, who'd just had her twelfth birthday, in pressing cold drinks on everyone and seeing that the pretty blue glass bowls of nibbles circulated freely. Soon chatter and laughter rang around the garden, and the children were tearing about getting loud and over-excited.

It was wonderful, this late-spring sunshine, Sarah thought contentedly. The lush grass, ideal for the children to tumble about on, was full of tiny pink and mauve wild-flowers which Marika told her the Germans called 'English Grasses'.

How lucky they were, she thought, gazing over the nearest field. Dwarf sunflowers were growing strongly, crowded together ready to flower in June and July when they'd lift their flat bronze heads each morning to follow the sun's arc across the sky. Behind them, dark pines marched green-black up the hills.

Five years ago, when Guy had been offered the job of senior transport manager of *GB Schwarz* in Germany, it had seemed a risk to sell their house in England and move to another country even if their new home was to be in this beautiful region, Bavaria. But the relocation package had been generous. The company not only made the move possible by providing this spacious house with its steeply pitched roof and chunky wooden balconies, they also paid for the girls to attend the nearby international school.

Guy's salary provided everything else they wanted – including having several other families along to help celebrate their wedding anniversary.

Sarah, happy to hold the domestic fort, had enjoyed preparing for the event. Despite their guests being from Denmark, Germany and America, she'd decided on very British party fare. Salad and cold meat, sausage rolls and things on sticks packed the fridge, waiting to be brought out to the long wooden table on the patio. Even so, she knew Guy would demand, 'But where's the *pork pie?*' Pork pies were made quite close to his parents' home in England and were a firm favourite with him, but some British delights simply couldn't be bought locally.

She glanced at her watch. For goodness sake, how much longer was Guy to be? And Josef?

Ellie ran up with four children around her. Ellie was always in the middle of everyone. 'Erika and Willem are *starving*. Can't we eat yet? I've been telling them all about the food.'

Sarah smiled at the expectant faces. 'I was hoping Dad would be here. But perhaps if we begin getting everything ready he'll have arrived by the time we've finished.'

While Ellie and her band of young but willing helpers debated noisily about the best arrangement of chairs, Sarah slipped into the house to phone Guy's office.

No answer. 'Oh well, that probably means he's already on the way home.'

She could begin setting out the food, *GB Schwarz's* offices were only half-an-hour away. He'd turn up any moment, pushing back his dark hair, beaming, shrugging off his jacket and throwing aside his tie.

She popped her head outside. 'Briony! I could use another pair of hands.'

Briony climbed slowly to her feet. No doubt she'd far rather have remained flopped in the dappled shade with Fabien, pretending the rest of the party didn't exist.

'Fab and me were talking about something,' she pointed out as she stepped into the roomy kitchen, nevertheless washing her hands in readiness to help.

'He'll live without you for ten minutes,' Sarah teased.

The table was laid, and the food crowded onto it somehow. One or two of the children grew tetchy at being kept waiting for their meal. Sarah grimaced. 'I think we'll begin, I can't think where Guy is but I'm sure he won't be long.'

'Puncture?' suggested Briony, lifting onto a chair one of the two Danish girls, little Mette, who was shy. Her more adventurous sister, Cecilie, scrambled onto a seat unaided.

'He wouldn't have forgotten, would he?' Ellie frowned.

'Of *course* not,' Sarah assured her. 'I'll put some food aside for him. I'll bet he'll be here in five minutes.'

In fact they were right at the end of the meal, polishing off chocolate cake, strawberry roulade and ice-cream by the time Guy did arrive. Suddenly he was there, in the doorway, wearing a dazed look almost as if he couldn't think what twenty or so people were doing on his lawn.

Sarah greeted him with a hug. 'Darling, are you all right?' His cheek felt clammy against hers.

13

He returned her hug mechanically. 'I've felt better.' He shrugged slowly out of his jacket. 'Perhaps I'll sit in the shade for a few minutes.'

She looked into his face anxiously. His deep brown eyes didn't meet hers. 'I've kept you some food...'

But he was shaking his head. 'I couldn't eat. Sorry.' He caught her hand for a moment and squeezed it.

Marika strolled across the grass, Hannah snuggled comfortably on her shoulder. 'You have not brought with you my husband?' She dipped to kiss Guy on each cheek. 'Do you always work so hard, you men? Such a long time today. And here your wife is having your anniversary party without you.'

'It couldn't be helped,' Guy replied, with a small smile.

The party fell curiously flat, then. Guy, having been so late, just sat in his chair like an old man, hardly talking, not eating, not even asking about pork pie. Sarah was disappointed that he didn't change into the soft cotton shirt which had been her gift to him.

And when their friends presented them with small gifts, she found herself expressing too profuse a gratitude in an effort to cover up his silence.

But the party didn't break up until the smaller children began to show their tiredness with complaints and occasional tears. And although she'd been looking forward to this day for weeks, Sarah wasn't altogether sad to see the guests go.

She saw them out in a flurry of thanks and promises to meet again soon. Briony and Fabien melted away and Ellie turned on the television.

The sun was dipping behind the hills and the garden fading into a lavender dusk. Guy sat exactly as Sarah had left him, having made no attempt to join her in waving everyone off. She felt a twinge of alarm. That was almost rude, most unlike Guy.

'Come and sit down.' His voice emerged from the twilight.

She took the seat beside him. It was chilly now, and she shivered. 'I ought to begin clearing up. Perhaps you should go to bed until you feel better?'

'I'm not ill.' He paused before taking a huge breath. 'Sarah, darling ... there's bad news.'

She turned quickly, searching his face, the face that she suddenly realised seemed creased with new lines. 'What?' Her mind whirled fearfully. 'Are you ill? Do you mean bad news from a doctor?'

He reached for her hand. 'Nothing like that.' Pulling himself wearily up in the chair, he shook his head slowly.

'Oh, Sarah,' he said quietly, tightening his hand on hers. 'I've lost my job.'

She stared, bewildered. 'Lost your job?' she repeated stupidly. 'How could that happen? You're excellent at your job, the *direktor* said...'

But he was shaking his head again. 'I haven't done anything wrong. It's all of us. Every one. *GB Schwarz* has gone under.'

For a few moments all Sarah could hear was a rushing in her ears. Then her own voice, hoarse in the gathering gloom. 'How? How could *Schwarz* go bust? They're respected, everyone knows them, they're an institution...'

He cut across her, wearily but with quiet finality. 'The authorities came in this afternoon. Men in suits and the police, the fraud people. They took away computers, whole cabinets of paperwork, and, for that matter, most of the directors, too. There are accusations of wrong-doing in the boardroom.'

'Oh no!' Sarah's voice snatched at her throat. 'And Josef?'

Guy nodded sombrely. 'Josef's job's gone,

too, of course. We're fortunate that neither of us are quite senior enough to be involved, viewed with suspicion. Because someone's been falsifying figures to look good for the investors and the banks. We've had to cease trading. I won't be going into the office except to make a statement.'

Darkness had crept up on them. Sarah realised she was shivering uncontrollably. She grasped Guy's arm with a fierce desire to exorcise the hopeless note from his voice. 'You don't deserve this, you've worked hard and you're *good* at your job. You'll get another...'

But he was shaking his head. 'I don't think so. Not in this country.' He gestured at the house. 'I'm afraid we can't stay here while I try. It belongs to *GB Schwarz*. The men in suits have told me to expect twenty-eight days to vacate.'

Jim Randle struggled for a moment with the heavy padlock on the yard gates, until finally the key grated round. His shoulders sagged. He was tired. So tired.

The yard seemed to have sucked the strength from him.

He turned to gaze at the heavy machinery which wasn't presently out on long-term

17

contract, motionless now at the end of the day, only the occasional ticking of a cooling engine to break the silence. Northampton-shire, in the middle of England, was a good place for a contracting firm. There was always something being built to make use of the artery of roads criss-crossing the country.

The business had been his life and livelihood. He knew it from the ground up, how much each digger or dump truck had cost, what it was worth now, whether there was finance still outstanding, where it would be working tomorrow and which driver would be operating it. He could operate every machine himself.

He knew every inch of tarmac that his plant machinery stood upon. He knew the state of the books in the small office within their bungalow at the side of the yard.

And he knew that it had all become too much for him. Far too much.

He trudged up to the red-brick bungalow. White and red petunias grown by his wife, Dinah, bedecked the frontage almost as if she were saying, 'The yard is ugly and I have to live beside it – but I will have my little piece pretty!' Just like Dinah, making the best of everything.

She was waiting for him now in the kitchen, wrapped up warm in a thick cardigan and comfy slippers. 'I thought you were never coming in. Dinner's ready – are you?'

'Certainly am. Smells wonderful,' he said, sinking heavily into his chair. The meal was delicious, but he didn't manage to empty his plate.

He sighed. 'It looks as if the time has come,' he remarked.

She stacked their plates absently. Her voice was gentle. 'It's for the best, Jim. The doctor's been warning you for long enough, you've known about your angina for years. Your body's telling you to slow up.'

He half-laughed. 'My body *has* slowed up! It's just my head and my heart which are still getting used to the idea.' He looked across at his wife. 'I suppose I'll have to see about putting the yard on the market,' he admitted gruffly. 'We'll have to talk about the bungalow. Are we going to keep it? Or sell it with the business?'

Dinah sighed, propping her chin on her hand. 'Oh dear, it *is* the end of an era! It's been our home for so long... But I don't know if I want to stay here with some stranger running the yard.'

'It's a funny thought, all right.'

19

'And you'd always be poking your nose into what the new owner was up to.'

They fell silent, contemplating some unpalatable truths. Jim heaved a sigh. 'So we have to find somewhere to live?'

They gazed at each other. It was difficult to image.

The bungalow was large for a couple, they'd built with plenty of room when the children were living at home, and had never felt the urge to move anywhere smaller.

'You go get your bath while I clear,' suggested Dinah. 'I suppose if you've got to give up the business then there are lots of decisions to make, but they'll wait another hour.'

Jim smiled suddenly at his wife. She was a woman with whom age had been kind. Her eyes were still young and peeped out of her face as if surprised to find themselves in the company of silver hair and less-than-smooth skin. But her movements were still brisk and she seldom complained of aches or stiffness.

He wished he could share her good health, but these days his limbs felt leaden, a day working a digger seemed endless, he had too little energy. And sometimes, at night, his breath wheezed and he felt as if the bulldozer had rumbled in from the yard to rest on his chest.

But he could hardly conceive of moving house.

It was *theirs*. Everything they'd chosen together, the cream kitchen units, the daffodil-lemon emulsion on the walls, the bright curtains

Dinah's voice roused him suddenly. 'Don't you nod off there, Jim Randle, I'm watching you! Get yourself bathed and I'll have a cup of tea waiting.'

He stretched and yawned. 'I hope you're not going to get bossy with me, just because I'm not so well.'

Dinah snorted. 'Someone needs to keep an eye on you.'

He climbed to his feet stiffly, just as the phone began to ring.

'Let me get it,' suggested Dinah. She liked to field evening calls to prevent too many people getting hold of Jim to chat about forthcoming jobs.

Jim hovered while Dinah announced, 'It's Guy!'

And then, at her increasingly dismayed side of the conversation, sat himself patiently down at the table again to listen. 'Just wait a moment while I tell Dad,' she said, eventually.

She took the phone from her ear. Her face was white, and suddenly she looked her age. 'Everything's gone wrong, that huge company he works for has gone bust, someone's been up to some funny business, apparently. Of course, their house goes with the job so they've got to clear out quickly. They're all terribly upset and worried. He wants to know if they can come and stay with us for a week or two while they sort themselves out.'

'There'll always be a home for them with us,' declared Jim.

Briony sat at a pavement café, pulled her jacket tightly around her and stared glumly into her orange juice, oblivious to the sights and sounds of the bustling town. 'Poor Dad,' she groaned. 'Why has this happened to him? He didn't do anything.'

Fabien grimaced, equally despondent. 'It is sad. Very bad. Some bad mans have made big trouble for everybody.'

She nodded. She didn't correct his English, her French being probably worse. They both spoke German fluently and often found it the most efficient method of communication between them.

'It puts pressure on us,' she grumbled. 'I

thought we had until August, and here we are, hardly into May and the family are rushing off "home". Not that England feels like home to me.'

'My home is France, always. Although I like it well, here.'

Briony smiled at Fabien, admiring his floppy chestnut hair blowing back from his face, the elegant way he folded his long body onto the small café chair. 'I can't wait for when you have a chance to show me France.'

'Me, also.' He smiled back, hazel eyes framed by thick lashes.

She sighed and drained her glass. 'So, do we have another drink? Or shall I go and talk to my poor family?'

Fabien pushed aside their glasses. 'First drink – a little red wine this time, perhaps? And family, then.'

Later, they caught the bus. Briony gazed through the window at neat fields and the pretty white houses, watching out for her favourite, a house with a painting in shades of sepia on the expanse of side-wall. An old woman carrying a sheaf of corn. 'I suppose I won't be seeing that painting much more, as we're leaving,' she sighed.

Fabien dropped a kiss on her neck. 'It's okay. We will be okay.'

'I know.' She turned and returned his kiss, earning a tut from an older woman sitting nearby.

His stop was before hers, near to the clinic where he'd been gaining experience towards medical school in France. After a last snatched kiss, he jumped down the step and waited on the pavement to wave as the vehicle drew away.

Although she smiled and waved, Briony felt her stomach contract a little as he disappeared. She wasn't particularly looking forward to talking to her parents. The *Schwarz* problem had made everything more difficult.

It was funny, she thought, hopping down at the end of their street, and watching the bus rumbling on its way, how she felt almost reluctant to enter the Randle home. She'd been so happy living in Mikhlut during her teens, getting the school bus into the suburbs of Munich, gaining friends of all nationalities. But since Dad had come home that night so grey-faced and stricken, the house seemed less welcoming, filled with packing cases, problem and despondent people.

It seemed a long time since Mum and Dad's party. Probably they wouldn't have any more parties in this house, ever.

'Hi,' she shouted, as she let herself into the tiled hall.

'In here,' called Dad's voice from the sitting room. 'Just having a breather. If we'd known we'd have to pack it all, we would never have bought you girls all the clothes we did!'

Both her parents were looking worn out, she noticed, but managed to keep on smiling for her and Ellie. She felt a pang of conscience. Mum had shadows beneath her grey eyes, and although always slender, seemed to have lost weight recently.

'Good job you didn't know then!' she retorted, joining in their banter. 'Would you like coffee?'

'Oh dear,' Mum teased. 'If you're *offering*, you must've done something terrible.'

'Not me,' Briony breezed, making hastily for the kitchen. 'Although,' she called back across the hall. 'I do want to speak to you.'

It seemed odd opening cupboards to see only half-a-dozen mugs where there had been towers of crockery. Most had already been packed into the boxes to be loaded into big vans in a couple of weeks, ready for a long-haul drive through Europe to England. Even though once they reached their destination there would be nowhere to put them.

She made the coffee carefully, one spoon of sugar for Dad, half-a-spoon for Mum, two spoons for herself, and carried the steaming mugs back in.

'Come on then, out with it,' Dad demanded, winking.

'And before you speak, just remember that money's become an issue,' Mum added, pushing back strands of her fair hair into the clasps she wore either side of her head.

Briony swallowed, then took a sip from her drink to lubricate her throat. 'Well, I have some news.'

Her parents waited.

She cleared her throat, and took another sip.

If she let the silence go on much longer, she'd never have the nerve to say it! She took a deep breath.

'I'm not coming back to England with you. I'm not going to university. I'm going with Fabien. We're going to work our way around France.'

Sarah felt as if she was going through her days beneath a huge black cloud.

Unbelievable. Incredible, how her happy

26

life had disintegrated in such a short time.

Guy's job was gone. The house would soon be gone. Ellie was trudging about with a tragic air of disbelief. They must leave all their dear friends, she felt as if she were missing Virginia and Marika already. No-one knew what lay ahead, if and when Guy – and herself, for that matter – would get a job, and where they'd settle.

And Briony wasn't coming home with them.

Briony *wasn't coming home with them!*

Her heart shrank. She alternated between despair at her daughter giving up her chance at one of the university places already provisionally offered, and anger at Briony's undisguised cheeriness and pleasure in her planned adventure. It seemed almost indecent in the face of the rest of the family's sadness.

She sighed and began to fill yet another bin-bag of clothes. They'd decided very early in the packing experience that they couldn't take everything with them.

Poor Guy, Briony's 'news' had been all he'd needed, hard on the heels of losing his job and their home. Sarah could still see the consternation on his already anxious face, the dismay.

'Work your way around France? But you hardly speak any French,' he'd snapped when their daughter dropped her bomb-shell. His voice held a note of finality, as if he expected that to end the matter.

Briony pointed out, 'I didn't speak *any* German when we came here. I learnt that, didn't I?'

His forehead puckered. 'But darling, you can't just rush off into the unknown! How will you live, what will you do? Where will you work?'

Their daughter had all the answers. Had apparently prepared more carefully for this interview than for any exam. 'We're going to Fabien's uncle's smallholding near Le Puy-en-Velay in Central France. We'll work there, and the house is big enough for them to offer us rooms in it. They grow lots of veg for the local markets and need extra help at the moment. It'll be a wonderful, simple life.'

'And what happens to you when Fabien goes back to medical school?'

Briony sipped her coffee thoughtfully. 'I don't think he's going to. I don't think it's what we want. He says you can have too much education.'

Guy snorted a scornful laugh, his eyes

angry and hard. 'No-one *ever* has "too much education"! As you'll find out if you intend to cobble together a "simple" life of casual work and the low pay which tends to go with it. It won't be much fun once the novelty's worn off. If you're not going to uni, can't you at least get a settled job with some prospects?'

Briony lifted her chin. 'That doesn't fit in with our plans.'

Sarah put her oar in hastily to give Guy a minute to cool off. 'Darling, can't you finish your education *first?* There are so many opportunities open to you. You could write to Fab and phone, and see him every holiday...'

Briony shrugged off this common sense. 'I'm eighteen. I'm an adult, and so's Fab. We've decided to make our own way in the world. We'll attend the University of Life.'

'I think you'll find it's the School of Hard Knocks,' Guy had returned bitterly.

With a huge sigh at the memory of his hurt concern, Sarah tied the bag up and began on another for old shoes and odd socks.

Guy was downstairs, making phone calls to UK contacts about the prospect of a job for when they arrived home in just over a week – *without Briony* her mind supplied. The whole *GB Schwarz* scenario was getting darker by the day. There was only the minimum severance pay, it looked suspiciously as if the staff's pension fund had disappeared, and word had spread through the industry that the company had harboured something very murky indeed.

Schwarz employees were being regarded with wariness. Which was unfair as only a very few of the board had been involved with the fraud which was haunting the newspapers' business pages.

Marika's husband, Josef, was gaining no better reception than Guy in his search for a new job. Marika called almost every day as she walked Hannah around Mikhlut. 'This is not right! Josef has not done wrong, not one thing. Everyone say, "it is a bad time now". It is bad time for Marika and Josef, true!'

'It's a bad time for Sarah and Guy, too,' Sarah would sigh, sympathetically. 'We're going to be homeless, soon! Marika, I *am* going to miss calling on you, shopping together, helping with Hannah. I've loved living here!'

She lugged the bag onto the landing, pausing to look out of the window, over the fields to the hills.

She wouldn't see the sunflowers open this year.

The village would go on without the Randles, they would miss the summer market and loud evenings at the Oktoberfest, Ellie wouldn't join in the Christingle service in the quaint village church when the youngest voices in the village would soar with Christmas magic.

They wouldn't be here to witness magnificent storms, thick hoar frosts, the snow.

She blinked hot eyes.

Instead they'd crowd into her in-laws' bungalow in the East Midlands with a view of the yard and Jim's precious diggers and dumpers. Guy would have no job, Ellie would have to begin a new school.

And Briony would be in France.

Briony - how could she bear to be so far from her daughter? How would she cope with the worry, the anxiety, the constant wondering whether Briony was okay?

She dashed her arm across her eyes quickly as Guy came up the stairs. 'Any luck?' she asked with false brightness.

He slid his arms around her. 'Only bad.' He blew out a slow, reflective breath. 'I've just been talking to a bloke about UK property prices.'

She tried not to let her despondency sound in her voice. 'And what did he say?'

'They've gone up – a lot – since we left.'

'Oh, well.' She tried the bright voice again. 'We've still got the money from the old house.'

'Mmm.' He leant his head on hers. 'But it's been invested. And investments have gone down.'

Four days later, Sarah was glad of Guy's arm around her once again as they stood at the coach station to wave off Briony and Fabien.

She watched Briony chattering to the driver, dark curls bobbing, as he stowed her two bright red suitcases in the belly of the coach, noted the brightness of her eyes and the spring in her step as she prepared to bound into a brand new life.

'Doesn't she mind parting from us at all?' Sarah whispered.

Guy nodded heavily. 'I don't think she does mind, not at this second. She's too caught up in herself and the prospect of the idyll she imagines.' He sighed. 'I hate this. I want her back and she hasn't even gone yet.'

Sarah sniffed. 'I think she *has* gone. In her mind and in her heart, anyway. We've lost her.'

The engine of the big, modern coach rumbled into life, and Briony, backpack bumping, rushed over, squeaking, 'We've got to go!'

Breathlessly, she gave Guy a big hug. Guy returned the embrace fiercely. 'Be sensible. And keep in touch. And remember that wherever you are, wherever we are, we'll always be your parents, and love you.'

'Yes, thanks,' Briony replied carelessly, and turned to Sarah.

Sarah felt the lithe body of her daughter in her arms, and felt physically unable to release her. Then Briony pulled away. 'Look after each other,' Sarah choked. She would have asked Fabien to look after Briony, but that was not this generation's way. Fabien generally seemed content to sit back and let Briony take the lead in their relationship.

''Bye then, 'bye Mum, 'bye Dad, 'bye Ellie! I'll phone you when we get there, then write to you at Gran and Granddad's! 'Bye!'

Briony almost danced up the stairs of the coach.

The rest of the Randle family gazed on in silence as the travellers found their seats and stowed their bags. Then they were waving, waving...

The silence seemed loud after the bus had pulled away.

Normally, Sarah enjoyed travelling by air. Usually trips to England were happy affairs of excitement and anticipation, usually the journey was spent chattering and making plans.

Usually they booked return tickets.

But not this time.

This time they travelled in gloom compounded by rain at Munich airport and mist at Heathrow. Ellie cut herself off by plugging into her personal stereo, Guy stared at the clouds, and Sarah flicked silently through a magazine.

After collecting their luggage, they had to make their way by train and then taxi, as Jim had said he was unable to meet them at the airport.

By the time the taxi passed beneath the *J R Randle Contracting* sign work was obviously over for the day. They pulled up before the bungalow.

Silence.

After the thrumming of the plane engines and then the noise of the car, the silence was a relief.

'Well, here we are,' Guy observed.

Sarah nodded dismally. Then she thought of Ellie's pinched, sad little face, and shook herself. 'Let's get inside and see Gran and Granddad, shall we Ellie?'

'Okay.'

Just then the door to the bungalow flew open and Guy sprang from the taxi to hug his mother and clap an arm around his father. Sarah realised, watching the joy on Jim's and Dinah's faces that they were just as glad to see Guy as she would've been if Briony had suddenly popped up. Parental love didn't dim with passing years, and having their daughters living nearby didn't mean they missed their son any less.

Jim, white hair blowing, and Dinah, smart and pretty in pastel colours, couldn't wait to usher them indoors. In no time they were all installed in their comfortable lounge, sipping tea and dunking biscuits.

Some of the first questions, naturally, were about Briony.

'Where is she?' demanded Dinah. 'All you said on the phone is that you'd explain when you saw us.'

Guy's expression stiffened. 'I'm afraid Briony has decided not to come back to

England. She's gone off to see a bit of France, to stay with some relatives of Fabien's for a while.'

'For the summer?' Dinah looked puzzled.

'Apparently not. She says they're going to "make their own way in the world"'

'She says she wants a simple life, living on farms and stuff, and she's had enough of education,' Ellie put in helpfully.

'Oh dear.' Dinah bit her lip. 'That's a bit ... headstrong.'

Jim, less tactful, snorted loudly. 'Foolish, you mean! Fancy throwing up a university place for some young French chap she's only known for months!'

Sarah hardly slept that night. Her mind was full of throbbing engines, packing, unpacking, Briony, Germany, Briony, Briony, Briony. The days ahead weren't appetising. Guy had to find a job, Ellie had to be got into a local school for the duration of their visit. Beside her, Guy slept.

At first light she rose to peep through the Regency-striped curtains into the yard. The men had turned up for work already. Jim, she saw, was amongst them. The raw-sounding engine of a digger barked into life.

Jim looked tired. He'd aged since they'd

visited at Christmas. Of course, Christmas and New Year were artificial times of holiday, good food, family, laughter. Now, in the cold light of day, Jim could be seen to be drawn, and heavy of movement.

Two diggers and two dumper trucks were manoeuvred onto low-loading lorries, then rolled ponderously away with the operators up in the cabs, leaving the yard quiet.

Jim stopped to speak to a man in the centre of the yard, then the man walked towards a big shed and Jim turned back to the bungalow.

Sarah gazed at the empty tarmac, cracked and rising in places with weeds and tree roots. At the lolling fence and the faded and patched sheds.

It wasn't much of a view compared to undulating fields and marching hills.

'Can't sleep?'

Sarah jumped. 'I thought you were asleep.'

'Not now.' Guy stretched.

Sarah realised suddenly how cold she'd grown in her bare feet, and scurried back to bed. It wasn't as big as the one at home – home? Not as big as their own in Germany, she meant – but she didn't mind. She could snuggle up to Guy, who was warm.

'I was watching Jim getting the machines

off. When he said he was taking today off, I didn't realise he'd have to get up at the crack of dawn to sort the men out, first.'

'I'm afraid he does a lot of that.'

'I hope it won't be too much for your parents, having us here.' Sarah sighed. 'Have you told them that we'll have to begin job-hunting straight away?'

'Yes, and that we can't afford to be fussy, not short-term, anyway. And I don't think they mind us being here. We don't want to use any more of our reserves than we have to, I need to find a job and we'll have to find a house in whichever area that proves to be.'

She turned things over in her mind, her head on his shoulder. They'd been churning exactly the same facts around for the past weeks, of course.

'Ellie's not happy at the thought of starting school on Monday. She hoped for a longer break.'

'Better if she bites the bullet and gets on with it,' he observed. 'We could be with Mum and Dad for weeks, months. She can't miss all that school.'

A door nearby opened and shut. Sarah lifted her head. 'Was that her getting up?'

Guy, more familiar with the sounds of the house, looked surprised. 'No. That was Dad going back to bed. Crikey, he's never done that before.'

Sarah found the days in the bungalow very long. Guy was either job-hunting or helping Jim. Sarah had little to do but help Dinah.

And think how little anyone said about Briony. They'd rung her at Fabien's uncle's smallholding near Le Puy, but had to time it well because the family finished work at dusk and were in bed soon after supper. Briony had sounded happy but distant. She was learning how to look after chickens, and hoe weeds.

Their furniture arrived in the big vans and Sarah was grateful to discover that Jim had had one of the two large sheds cleared and cleaned to accommodate it, so at least they didn't have to pay for storage.

They saw Mrs Drage, the head teacher of the local comprehensive, a huge school of mis-matched buildings. Mrs Drage admitted Ellie Randle immediately to year eight, and Sarah and Guy left her in the care of a girl from that year.

Sarah went for a walk while Guy went back to the yard, up lanes hedged with grass and soap-smelling hawthorns, into the country where the fields were full of oilseed, wheat or corn, but no sunflowers.

Then she returned to wait for Ellie to come home from school. But when she saw the way her daughter trudged across the yard she felt her heart sink. 'How did it go, sweetheart?'

Ellie didn't even pause on her way to her room. 'That was the most horriblest day of my life,' she stated succinctly.

Oh dear!

Sarah found things to occupy her for half-an-hour, then tapped and went into Ellie's room, taking a mug of Ellie's favourite hot chocolate. Ellie lay on her bed listening to her personal stereo.

Sarah gently removed the earphones. 'What was so awful?'

Ellie looked away.

Sarah kissed her daughter's forehead. 'I can't help you if you won't talk.'

Ellie blew out a sigh like a dragon. 'I don't know anyone and it's just so *huge*. No-one was nice, or wanted to talk. I didn't know where I was supposed to go, and some girls laughed.'

'Maybe you were meant to laugh, too?' She stroked Ellie's hair.

'Huh!'

'A new school's tough,' Sarah acknowledged. 'Things are hard for all of us.'

'*Briony* seems okay,' Ellie said with sudden vehemence.

'Well, I hope she is.' Sarah tried to make her voice reasonable. 'I wouldn't want her to be unhappy. She's far away, in another country like we were in Germany.'

'*This* is another country! Germany is home.'

A couple of weeks passed, Ellie said little about school other than "'S' all right,' Guy filled in applications, Sarah filled her days as best she could. Then Jim and Dinah asked to 'have a chat' with Guy and Sarah. Jim appointed himself chairman of the meeting which took place over a teapot and a plate of jam tarts.

'No luck on the job front?'

Guy looked uncomfortable. 'It's early days, Dad. I've had a couple of interviews and the agencies I've signed up with are quite hopeful that it'll come together for me soon. I've been sending out applications'

His father looked at him.

Guy grimaced and sighed. 'No luck on the job front yet, no.'

'Right.' Jim looked around the table. 'Well, what we want to talk about is this: I'm afraid we have a problem, too.'

Sarah looked from Jim to Guy, whose face had creased with concern. 'What?' Guy demanded sharply.

'I have to give up work.' Jim thrust out his chin as if expecting an argument about it. 'I'd expected to go on for another five or even ten years, but my angina's getting worse, and the doctor said I have to stop. We decided to sell the business. And your mother and me, we decided that if we're going to sell the business, we'd better sell the bungalow, because we wouldn't want to sit here staring at strangers in "our" yard.'

Guy looked thunderstruck. 'I'm sorry, Dad,' he said simply. 'This must be very hard.' He scratched his head. 'Of course, we'll move out as soon as possible, I'm sure it won't be very long before I find something.'

His father nodded. 'I'm sure it won't, either. That's why I want to snap you up before someone else does.'

'Snap me up?' Guy looked amazed.

Jim grinned. 'How would you like to take over the business?'

Chapter Two

'I never thought I'd be doing this – going to work in Dad's yard!' Guy tightened the laces of his new work boots. 'He was always trying to get me interested in his diggers when I was younger, but I had my own ideas.'

Sarah grimaced. She was perched on the edge of the bed, a thin green dressing gown around her shoulders against the chill of an early morning in June, the light thin and grey, the sun not long up. 'You could always tell Jim you don't want to take over the business. He'll understand. It's your decision, he realises there are other things you'd rather do.'

'But he also understands that I've already tried to find employment in "other things" since we came back from Germany. And failed. I used to believe that a good man could always get a job in sales...' He knew his voice was flat with disappointment, but the way the world was treating them didn't seem fair. He lay awake at night brooding over *GB*

Schwarz, the old job, their old home, how property prices had gone up and investments dwindled while they'd been away.

He heard Sarah give a tiny sigh and hated the knowledge that she was disappointed, too.

'Perhaps we should remember what Briony always says,' she observed. 'There are no problems – only challenges.'

Guy found his throat too tight to reply. Briony. His heart lurched every time he thought about her, far away in France.

Going to the mirror, he stared at his own reflection. How peculiar it felt to dress for work in a casual chequered shirt and jeans. In his imagination he overlaid the image with himself preparing for a day in the glassed-in offices of *GB Schwarz.* In those days he'd put on a crisp shirt, a tie, a well-pressed suit. One of the same suits which hung empty in the wardrobe now. 'I've only had two interviews,' he continued, turning away.

'You've only been looking for a few weeks,' Sarah pointed out, yawning.

'I've tried to tell myself that, too, but it isn't much comfort. I've certainly been able to get ... well, the *flavour* of what to expect. That polite wariness when I admit I've been out of the UK market for several years and have no reference from my previous employers because they went bust in the midst of a fraud! Also, I'm...' He halted abruptly, not having meant to frame his next thought in words.

Sarah frowned, rising, her long fair hair fuzzy from the pillow, her feet bare on the bedroom carpet. A good-quality carpet, but beige, a 'safe' colour they'd never have chosen themselves. Their own things were stored away, carved furniture and richly-coloured rugs.

'Also?' she prompted softly.

He sighed as he looped his arms around her. His voice dropped ruefully. 'Also, Sarah, *I'm middle-aged!*'

He watched a smile widen her mouth, suppressed laughter brimming in her eyes. 'I know darling. Me, too. But I've been hoping you wouldn't notice.'

He returned her smile glad, despite everything, that she could see some humour in their situation. 'Employers seem to want everyone to be in their twenties and preferably fresh from some university. I'd love to walk into another sales manager's position with a salary large enough to support us all and a mortgage, but ... it just seems so unlikely.' He pushed his fingers through his hair. '*J R Randle Contracting* has given Mum and Dad a good living for long enough. If I take over it'll support us, and we'll be able to hang on and wait until we've accumulated a bit more money before looking for a house. Until then...'

'Until then we stay put,' she acknowledged. 'And it's good of your mum and dad to have us.' All signs of amusement faded. Her eyes locked intently on his. 'But Guy, I don't want you to do a job which makes you unhappy!'

He tightened his arms around her, taking comfort from her heartbeat, the warmth of her body against his. He kissed her. 'But I'm unhappiest with no job at all.'

In a few minutes he was walking into the kitchen where his parents were already eating breakfast, his father, Jim, in similar work-wear to himself, his mother, Dinah, passing out hot, buttery toast. Guy made sure his smile was big and enthusiastic. ''Morning, Guy Randle, newest member of the workforce reporting for duty!'

Jim beamed. He looked ruddier and more relaxed as if just the prospect of his son taking on the day-to-day running of the yard was enough to improve his health. 'And it's

46

marvellous, boy! Delighted to have you.'

Guy had no doubt about it, Jim's face shone with pleasure. But all the beaming smiles in the world didn't quiet his qualms.

More than his clothes felt odd this morning, more than getting up so early ready to send the machinery out.

But perhaps the wriggles of doubt and pangs of anxiety were down to the fact that he simply didn't know the business. *Yet!* he amended inwardly. *I don't know the business properly yet.*

When he stepped out into the yard at Jim's side he gazed at the tarmac, the plant and the tool-hire shed with new eyes. Till now all this had been his father's area of expertise, something Guy had only a general picture of. Now was the time to involve himself and fill the gaps in his knowledge.

Of course, he'd been up on a digger or a dump truck before, he'd been brought up with the roaring, clattering yellow monsters, but he was well aware of his deficiencies and that his new role was going to be a pretty hands-on experience. 'I'll have to make the arrangements to get some proper training,' he thought aloud.

Jim patted the enormous ribbed tyre of the nearest digger. 'The digger course isn't bad, but your heavy goods licence will probably take longer. You'll do it, boy.' He thrust a clipboard into Guy's hands. 'First things first, we've two machines going out on contract this morning. Ron'll be here any moment, you need to check with him he's seen those machines are ready. The large rotavator's running rough and needs attention because it's got to be delivered to a customer by ten, then we need to speak to that site at Astley Meadow...'

Jim started off across the yard with long strides and a frown of concentration, waving his arms and listing enough jobs to keep them busy until Christmas. Calmly, Guy held his ground, flipping over the pages on the clipboard.

Jim halted. Looked round.

'Aren't you supposed to be resting?' Guy called mildly.

His father looked uncomfortable, tucking his hands disconsolately in his pockets and retracing his steps more slowly. 'S'pose so.'

Guy studied Jim's face, the lines of tiredness, the shortness of breath. He struggled for the right words. 'I know there's a lot for me to learn, Dad, but I *do* know how to talk to Ron and Tom. And there won't be anyone at the site office at Astley for at least an hour. If you're going to gallop about the yard exactly as you've always done there's no point in me being here, because you'll just make yourself ill anyway.'

Jim shuffled his feet and heaved a jagged sigh. 'I can't just *stop.*'

Although the doctor had been quite definite that he must do that exact one thing because Jim's angina was a symptom of heart disease, Guy knew better than to put that into harsh words. 'Of course you can't' he agreed, instead. 'Just slow down for now, leave the rushing about to me. For a start you could have another cuppa while I sort these jobs out and see the men are okay, then I'll come in and we can go through what needs doing next, ring the transport training company and Astley Meadow.'

'Oh, all right.' Jim turned and scuffed slowly towards the house, adding, under his breath, 'Young bossy boots.'

Guy just grinned, aware of the wisdom of allowing his father get the final word, and turned to greet the mechanic, Tom, as he whizzed his little red motor scooter in through the gates. Soon he was deep in consultation with chatty, cheerful Tom, and the older, more taciturn Ron.

It was a long day, the first of many. Guy

got used to the lengthy hours and then the phone ringing just as he thought he might sit down to dinner. He got used to his working day being supervised by his father. And he got used to the noise, the dust. By the end of a couple of weeks he was even beginning to enjoy the sense of purpose.

Naturally, there was a lot to learn about the machinery, the clients, the men, the paperwork and the idiosyncratic work methods of Pauline, the lady who came into the office for a couple of days each week to deal with it. But at least he knew he'd taken a load off Jim's shoulders already and ensured his father got plenty of breaks.

He'd applied for his provisional licence and booked the theory test for long goods vehicles. Operating a digger involved more than on-site work, he had to be licensed to move it along public roads. When he got a minute he practised his digger manoeuvres within the confines of the yard, and had only one small mishap – discovered at Ron's anguished cry of, 'Oy! You've squashed my lunch!'

Sarah squeezed into the little office in the tight space between bulging filing cabinets and heaped shelves.

Immediately she realised that she'd picked a bad time to try and speak to her husband. Guy was in discussion with Pauline, queen of *J R Randle's* paperwork, and it sounded as if things weren't going smoothly. Oh dear! Only weeks into Guy's new job and already he was running into staff problems.

'I'm sorry, Pauline,' Guy said to the woman perched on the only chair, a little frown on her face. 'But I'm afraid a proper computer is coming to this business, something far more versatile than this old word processor you prepare contracts on. Your ledgers are beautiful, but a computer will be better for the books – books, estimates, correspondence, contracts, the lot.'

'But I've no idea how to use a proper computer,' Pauline declared, with finality.

Sarah watched her husband's eyes narrow. 'Training will be arranged. I should've mentioned it earlier.' Guy always became coldly courteous when he was crossed and Sarah could've warned Pauline not to waste her breath in argument.

Pauline did though, as she flipped open one of her beautiful, hand kept ledgers, saying dismissively, 'I think I'm too old for all this change, at over fifty, don't you?'

'Not at all,' Guy persisted with awful

politeness. 'You're an intelligent, competent person, and I have every confidence that you're capable of learning. And that, I'm afraid, is what I have to ask you to do.'

Sarah slipped out again, she'd talk to Guy later.

She was unsurprised, but still dismayed, to learn, when he appeared later, that Pauline had given a week's notice. 'Oh dear, perhaps she'll change her mind when she's had a chance to mull it over?'

Guy blew out his cheeks, shrugging. 'Doubt it. I did ask her several times to reconsider, she's known the business for years which is very valuable. But her son's been on at her to work for him, so our new computer has unfortunately been the deciding factor. No doubt Dad'll have something to say about how the office has always worked perfectly well without a computer.' He slung his arm around Sarah's shoulders. 'I don't suppose I could interest you in the job, could I?'

Sarah felt her heart plunge. Certainly, she'd declared her intention of getting a job, had even begun scanning the evening paper.

But she'd anticipated choosing something to which she felt drawn, work she'd enjoy in pleasant surroundings. Perhaps in a bright little shop where she'd meet lots of people. She'd done a part-time job in a small office before and not found it very stimulating. She had no up-to-date computer experience either, although she could find her way around the elderly family machine okay.

'Wouldn't you rather get someone whizzy, who knows exactly how accounts are done electronically?'

He pulled a face. 'I'd rather have you. You won't be any trouble.'

'Oh. Well ... okay, I suppose.' It wasn't the most gracious job offer she'd ever had, but perhaps she ought to do her bit. Probably the last thing Guy needed at the moment was to have to embark on the business of advertisements and interviews.

She tried not to contrast the idea of working alone in that little overstuffed cupboard of an office with her memories of her old life in the pretty village of Mikhlut. There, her days had been built around domestic and family responsibilities, of course, but also she'd found time for getting out and about, shopping, visiting friends. She felt a great tug of regret as she thought of her best friend, Marika, and her husband Josef, wondering whether Josef's search for work had been any easier than Guy's. And baby

Hannah must've grown by now, would be able to hold a rattle and grin big, gummy grins.

And, of course, when they'd lived in Mikhlut they'd still had Briony...

'Great!' Guy gave her a quick hug then hurried to the door to the yard, leaving behind him, 'The computer should be delivered on Friday. Someone's coming to set it up and I expect they'll give you a few tips.'

'Oh good,' she replied to the space he vacated. 'Looks like I start work on Friday, then, doesn't it? Good old computer.'

The family ate together in the dining-room, a staid room of ivory and crimson. Over a supper which Sarah cooked, a rich steak casserole with a mouth-watering aroma, the subject of the computer arose again. And at least one person was thrilled – Ellie.

Her brown eyes lit up. *'Mega!'* she breathed. 'And it'll be connected to the Internet, won't it? So I'll be able to e-mail all my friends in Germany! Wow! That'll be wicked, I can't wait to hear from Willem and Erika and...'

'Just a moment, young lady.' Jim peered at his granddaughter sternly. 'I don't remember you being given permission to touch this expensive machine, do you? What would a girl your age know about computers, anyway?'

'More than anyone else in the house,' Sarah thrust in quickly, seeing Ellie's face darken dramatically and fearing an outburst which would give Jim the perfect excuse to further lay down the law. 'In fact, I'm relying heavily on Ellie to show me how to put the books on it, she's worked with spreadsheets at school. So if she's allowed to use the e-mail it'll be a fair exchange, don't you think?'

'That's all right, Mum.' Ellie let her hair slide down to hide an angry face as she dropped her knife and fork, her meal only half-eaten. 'I'll help you, I don't need anything in exchange. May I leave the table? I've got loads of homework.'

Jim expostulated, 'But you haven't finished! Your mother's cooked a lovely meal...'

'Yes, you may,' Sarah replied quietly.

After that the gathering was subdued. Sarah lost her own appetite, unhappy at the way her father-in-law had leapt on Ellie. She sighed inwardly. Misunderstandings were a feature of several generations living together, she supposed.

For an instant she closed her eyes, missing again their own home and all their friends...

Friends! She sat up, remembering why she'd searched Guy out earlier in the day. 'Shelly Manton phoned, she used to work with me in Northampton, do you remember? She has two daughters, Jessica and Caitlin. They live in Norwich now and she's invited us for the day, on Sunday.'

Guy frowned. 'I don't know about that, there's always something to do...'

His mother, until then a quiet, silver-haired presence at the top of the table, cut across him. 'That will fit in with us beautifully. I'd like Jim to have a quiet day, which he won't if you're pottering about the yard, Guy, and it'll do you good to get off on your own, meet your old friends and forget the business for a while. It's a mistake to live for the business seven-days-a-week.'

Sunday was beautiful, one of those occasional perfect summer days. A fresh blue sky gleamed above fields packed with the vibrant yellow of oilseed and pale green of unripe corn as if someone had laid massive carpets over the hills, and the birds seemed to flute especially clear and beautiful songs.

They reached Norwich in time for lunch. It was lovely to meet up with jolly, comfortable Shelly and the girls again. Ellie disappeared upstairs immediately with Caitlin and Jessica, swapping loud opinions about music and hair styles as their feet clumped up the stairs, and Sarah was delighted to observe her daughter's shining eyes and hear her happy voice.

For herself, it was just a relief to plump down in the sitting room with a cup of tea and forget their 'challenges' for now, to enjoy the delicious smell of lasagne and garlic bread wafting from Shelly's kitchen, and to catch up on Shelly's life since the days when they were work-mates.

After lunch they walked into Norwich city centre to admire the grace and dignity of the Guildhall and City Hall and the ancient staunchness of the castle. The market, with its brightly-striped awnings, was shut on a Sunday, but the girls found plenty of shops to explore.

Regretfully, at five, Sarah looked at her watch. 'Ellie's got school tomorrow...'

Guy sighed, but nodded. 'I must be up early, too.'

For most of the drive home Ellie cut herself off with the earphones of her lilac-coloured *Schwarz* personal stereo, gazing through the window, head nodding in time to her music.

The heat was fading from the day's sun by the time they drew up in the yard in front of the long, brick-built bungalow and Dinah's tubs of jolly petunias already beginning to cascade down to the floor. Sarah had surprised herself by dozing for most of the two hours of the journey. She yawned and stretched. 'I dropped off! Must be something to do with my age.'

Ellie spoke from the back seat. She'd made no move to get out of the vehicle and there was no sign of the earlier joy in her voice. 'Are we going to live with Gran and Granddad for much longer?'

Sarah turned. 'For now, anyway. Why?'

There was something in her daughter's eyes, lighter, more golden versions of Guy's. Ellie held her gaze for a moment, then away. 'Oh. Nothing.' Then with sudden animation, 'Look! There's a *dog!* Isn't he gorgeous?'

Sarah twisted round further to look. 'I wouldn't describe him as "gorgeous". "Odd", perhaps, or "enormous". The way his coat curls all around his face, and with those soup-plate paws, he looks half cart-horse, half teddy bear.'

Guy grinned. 'Better get him out of the yard before I lock the gates.'

But the moment he opened the car door the dog spun and whipped away, flattening himself to wriggle into a space under the tool-hire shed.

Ellie giggled. 'He's hiding from you, Dad!'

Guy ruffled her hair. 'Well, I'm certainly not going to wriggle in after him. He'll come out when he's ready, I suppose.'

They'd scarcely been indoors five minutes when Sarah noticed Ellie slipping out of the kitchen door with a handful of biscuits. She moved to the window to watch.

First Ellie crouched to peer into the space under the shed. Then she backed off, dropping a biscuit on the floor and retreating to the bungalow steps. After a couple of minutes the dog reversed out of his hidey-hole. He stood for a moment, ears poking up through his extravagant, golden coat, head cocked. Then he inched forward and ate the biscuit in one snatch.

Ellie threw him another piece. This time the dog wagged his frondy tail as he ate, then advanced a few steps with a hopeful doggy grin, all caution apparently abandoned. Within minutes he was snuffling down the last crumbs from Ellie's hand and Sarah could hear her daughter encouraging him. When the biscuits were all gone the dog frisked in circles, chin in and chest out, tail and back one continuous wiggle. Ellie laughed with delight and jumped up to skip around with him.

Deciding not to warn Ellie about be-friending unknown dogs just this once, Sarah turned instead to help Dinah in the kitchen.

Ellie ran in when called for a late tea. 'The dog's got a collar on but no name tag. I think he must be a stray.'

Jim helped himself to ham, and pork pie. 'Lost, I should think. Strays don't normally wear a collar. We let the police know he's here when he turned up this afternoon, but he hasn't been reported missing.' He passed the plate of pork pie to Guy, who took two pieces.

Ellie's face brimmed with hope. 'If no-one claims him, can I have him? He's so friendly and happy, he pulls funny faces and wags his tail and I'd love...'

Sarah broke in hurriedly, interrupting her daughter's wiggling demonstration of how the dog looked when it wagged its tail. 'Don't set your heart on that, darling, prob-ably someone *will* claim him. Anyway, it's a bit much to expect Gran and Granddad to put up with having an enormous funny-looking dog foisted on them.' With a sinking heart, she watched the light fade from Ellie's eyes.

Jim nodded. 'A dog that size would need to be walked miles.'

'I'd walk him,' Ellie insisted.

'You say that now, but it's a big responsibility.'

'But....!'

Dinah spoke composedly over whatever Ellie had been about to burst out with. 'I expect Sarah's right and he will be claimed, but, funnily enough, I was thinking that if the police didn't trace his owner I'd rather like him for myself. Walking him would be such good exercise. Perhaps Ellie and I could have joint ownership?' She winked at her granddaughter. 'He looks really cuddly, doesn't he? As if someone knitted him.'

Dinah volunteered herself and Jim for the washing-up to give the others a rest after their day out.

'It's the first I've heard of you wanting a dog!' Jim snorted, the moment they were alone.

Serenely, Dinah rinsed the plates. 'We used to have dogs, didn't we? He might guard the yard, too.'

Jim opened the drawer and took out a fresh tea-towel. 'Guard? That lolloping thing? He's not a year old, I'll bet, he wouldn't know how to guard his own biscuit.'

Laughing, Dinah began filling up the washing-up bowl, watching the water froth up into white bubbles. 'He'll learn.'

Jim thrust out his chin the way he did when he wanted to make a point. 'And young Ellie ought to learn that she can't have everything she asks for.'

Dinah didn't respond immediately, but washed-up several plates with thoughtful thoroughness before musing, 'Jim, aren't you being a bit hard on Ellie? She's been uprooted from everything she knew, lost all her friends and had to begin in a very different type of school. I believe it might be good for her to have a dog to love. And to add to all that you seem to jump on her whenever she opens her mouth – what's the problem?'

Jim looked surprised. 'Do I? I don't mean … well, I just think those girls were given too much freedom, and look what happened with Briony as a result!'

Dinah dropped the plate she was washing back into the water, and turned, drips dropping from her fetching pink rubber gloves. 'What exactly has Briony done wrong?'

Her husband's mouth hung open for a moment in surprise. 'You know very well! She went off to France with some boyfriend instead of coming back to England to study at university. All that schooling down the drain, an opportunity like that thrown away...'

Dinah narrowed her eyes. 'I asked, what did Briony *do wrong?*' Jim looked puzzled and fell silent. Dinah kept her eyes on him. 'The answer is "nothing"! She's an adult who chose to work abroad – for a while or forever, it doesn't matter. It's not against the law, is it?'

Jim considered, whisking his tea-towel. He didn't quite meet her eyes. 'N-o.'

'No. She may go to university next year or in ten years or never. She may live here, she may live there. That's her choice. It's her life.'

She turned back to her dishes. 'Even if Briony does do something foolish, being strict with Ellie isn't going to change that. And Ellie has two perfectly good parents living with her, I don't think *we* need to concern ourselves with correcting her behaviour. It's actually none of our business how much freedom the girls may have been given.'

With a sigh, Jim tossed his tea-towel on the table, smoothing down his white hair, a worried gesture Dinah knew only too well. 'I didn't mean to be tough on Ellie. It's just that I'm worried about Briony. Will she be okay? Will the family of that boyfriend treat her well? Has she got enough money?'

Dinah pulled off her gloves and threaded her arms around him. 'I know! I feel exactly the same. And so do Guy and Sarah, of course. However much they might try to hide it.'

'No more work today, yes?'

Briony shouldered her hoe with relief, and grinned at Fabien. 'Is it time to stop? Thank goodness for that.' She looked back in satisfaction at the clear earth between the long rows of squashes in shades of orange and cream, stripping off her gloves, careful of her blisters.

Fabien waited for her to fall into step beside him. 'Tante Rose makes dinner. Fish, I think.'

She took his hand. 'Mmm, that sounds lovely. Aunt Rose is a great cook.' Rose was a typical countrywoman, plain and sensible in the way she wore her hair and dressed, used to hard work about the smallholding,

64

or 'fermette' as it was called, and quick about her domestic chores.

They stowed their tools before going into the house. There was just time to wash their hands before the meal was on the table, fish pie with a breadcrumb topping and cheese sauce, served with leeks and kale.

'*Merci beaucoup,* Tante Rose.' Briony smiled as she took her place. Aunt Rose smiled back and passed Briony a brimming plate.

After grace, Aunt Rose, Uncle Ferdinand and Fabien carried on a gentle conversation in French. Briony had stopped minding about not being included. Fabien's aunt and uncle spoke no English and seemed as foxed by Briony's schoolgirl French as she was by their rapid, colloquial speech, their being much broader than Fabien's.

She couldn't say she felt close to Fabien's aunt and uncle although they fed her well and were kind enough in an absent way, and she was bright enough to realise they would've been content for Fabien to visit them alone, as he had other summers. Fabien knew the work of the fermette and could really help, lifting, picking and packing the produce gently so as not to spoil it.

Briony was well aware of having no experience of working on the land, and could scarcely tell a runner bean from a pea-pod. Idiot-proof work was therefore allocated to her and she felt she knew how to hoe now and heap up the long stalks of the leeks to keep them white. She'd certainly got her wish of a simple life, because the work didn't exactly test her brain.

She tried to smother a yawn. The long days and physical work often had her drooping over her dinner, but tonight she had plans other than just falling into her little bed with the rose-splashed quilt. Today was Friday and she and Fabien were going into the town of Le-Puy-en-Velay to meet friends.

Briony loved Le Puy, as well as being a beautiful cluster of mediaeval buildings on the slopes of two volcanic peaks, one occupied by the stately statue Notre-Dame-de-France known locally, and with affection, as 'The Red Lady'. Le Puy was friendly and jolly and she wished the fermette wasn't quite so far out so they could visit more often. But on Fridays they could usually get a lift with a neighbour and descend on their favourite café not far from the cathedral to drink strong coffee and rough red wine.

Fabien being easily distracted by lengthy

conversations with Rose and Ferdinand, it was normally up to her to make sure they got to the road on time to pick up their lift. But, to her, it was worth the effort.

With people her own age, between her French and their English she found she could communicate, and she wasn't going to miss the opportunity of an evening away from the fermette.

Claire, Nicole, Jean and the others were waiting for them when they arrived at *Café Berac,* the tables and chairs spilling out onto the pavement. 'Allo!' they called. 'You are almost too late, we eat ice-cream!' And they all waved chocolate-dipped cones.

Briony quickened her pace at the sight of the ice-cream salesman with his little push-cart. He sold a rich caramel-and-nut con-coction of which she was particularly fond. Even though they didn't have a lot of spare money they could afford such an extrava-gance on an occasional night out.

In a minute they'd made their purchases and dropped into vacant chairs to order sweet, frothy coffee to go with them.

The evening was already navy blue and the outside of the café was dotted with tiny lights which cast a golden glow. The group of youngsters were in high spirits and the mixed English-and-French conversations rang out, woven with shrieks of laughter. Briony followed most of it. It was only when her attempts at French were met with Rose and Ferdinand's politely blank expressions that she became tongue-tied.

Nicole spoke the best English of the group and enjoyed exhibiting her prowess. 'And when is it that you must take another job?' she asked Briony, late on into the evening.

Briony frowned. Stuck for Nicole's meaning, she hesitated.

Nicole turned to Fabien and asked the same question in French.

With a shrug, Fabien drained his drink. '*Une semaine.*'

Briony caught that, all right. 'One week?' She turned to him in bewilderment. 'Another job in one week? What do you mean?'

He smiled and flung his arm around her, waving away her concern with an expressive hand. 'The work with Rose and Ferdinand, one week more. Then we find work again.'

She pushed his arm away. '*Why?* Don't we work hard enough? Is it me?' Her aching back and shoulders suggested to her that she was industrious enough for anyone, but she did always feel like the weak link.

He roared a forced, artificial laugh. '*Non.*

68

No, of course, no. We work for six weeks here, that is all. That is the job.'

'It is the season, you understand,' Nicole supplemented. 'Now there will be a break until the fruit is ready to come from the trees, later. And in this break Rose and Ferdinand work alone.'

Briony nodded slowly. 'So they're in a lull. Just this year? Or every year?'

'Every year.' Fabien lifted his glass and caught the waiter's eye. He seemed finished with the subject, but Briony was not so easily satisfied.

When they were set down by the kind neighbour with his old black car on the road outside the smallholding at the end of the evening, she held him back from entering the house. 'What on earth is going on?' she whispered. 'I thought we had jobs here as long as we wanted them! How long have you known that it was for such a short season?'

He yawned. 'Always it is so.'

'Why didn't you tell me?' she demanded furiously.

He did a big, French shrug. 'I think you comprehend. Always it is so. Each year.'

Briony brushed past him to go inside, angry and upset. There was something about Fabien's explanation, either ingenuousness or an element of evasion, which sat badly with her. Back in Germany when he'd suggested she join him in this idyll it had been about living and working with his relatives. She'd assumed it would be an on-going arrangement.

They hardly had enough money even when board-and-lodging was provided by Rose and Ferdinand. What were they supposed to do next?

She worked in silence all the next day, worried and hot in the sun. After dinner, Fabien steered her outside for an evening walk. He seemed anxious to improve the atmosphere between them. 'The friends of my uncle need assistants on their land. Marius and Honoriane near Retournac. They have a different season.'

She studied his face, lit only on one side in the moonlight. 'Fabien, did you deliberately mislead me?' The sentence was too difficult to get over in English or for her to translate into French, so she repeated it in German, the one language they each spoke well.

'Of course not! This work is always for a certain time, that's all. We must move on. Shall I tell Marius that we will be his assistants? And,' he added hastily, 'ask for how many weeks he needs help?'

Briony nodded slowly.

Before long she was packing her cases again. Uncle Ferdinand was kind enough to give them a lift to the fermette near Retournac, and motoring along a road beside the Loire River, every turn affording another pretty view, Briony let the lush, rolling greens lift her spirit.

But they were soon to plummet when they finally reached the home of Marius and Honoriane.

She hoped her face didn't mirror her horror.

Where Ferdinand and Rose's property had been all neatly painted, the buildings here were grey and grimy, the sheds and barns a patchwork of boards, corrugated iron and sheets of plastic. A flock of turkeys corralled near to the house beside a yard full of weeds kept up a constant high-pitched babble, and gave off a pungent smell.

Indoors was no better. Worse, in fact. Briony stared in dismay at the untidy, grubby kitchen where a chicken perched comfortably on the back of a chair. Worse, the room she was allocated proved to be a meagre cobwebby little space with tired-looking sheets and a threadbare quilt left for her to make up the bed. The sunlight could barely filter through the dusty window panes.

She turned to Fabien in mute appeal. He shrugged apologetically as he followed their new employer down to his own room.

Briony gazed at the ripped vinyl flooring, the grey walls, the layer of dust over everything. How was she going to live here? It was horrible.

Chapter Three

Briony flung open one of her cases and rummaged until she found an old tee-shirt which had long ago washed out from purple to tired pink, then marched down to the elderly, far-from-sparkling bathroom. There she appropriated a large tin jug that she filled with warm water and carried back to her room.

Then she sorted through her backpack until she found her shell-pink *Schwarz* personal stereo and a favourite disc. For a second, holding the familiar object in her hands she felt a huge wave of homesickness for her parents and their comfortable life together in Germany, remembering the pride she'd felt at her father's senior position in the multi-national company, *GB Schwarz*. Senior sales manager, Guy had been delighted to see *Schwarz's* marketing working on the target, teenage market – all her friends at school in Munich had sported a trendy, must-have *Schwarz* personal stereo in one of a rainbow of pastel colours, with the slogan, *Schwarz muss nicht schwarz sein...* Black doesn't have to be black.

And grey didn't have to be grey, she decided, looking distastefully around the cobweb-bedecked room she'd been allocated at the smallholding of Marius and Honoriane. Well, she wasn't going to put up with it! She plunged her old tee-shirt in the water to become her cleaning cloth, poured in some shampoo in lieu of a more effective cleaner, clamped on her earphones and set about making her living space habitable, or at least bearable, letting the music lend her work a rhythm. The water had to be changed often as she took her wrung-out cloth to cobwebs, dust and grime, the windows, the little table which looked as if it might once have been part of a treadle sewing machine, the dull, dark chest with ill-fitting drawers, the headboard, even, gingerly, the bare bulb hanging on a wire from the ceiling.

By the time she was washing the floor – the vinyl proved to be blue – Fabien had arrived to watch disconsolately from the doorway.

'My room also,' he said gloomily, as Briony scrubbed, her hair flopping irritatingly in her eyes. 'It is ... not so nice.'

Briony wrung out her cloth for the millionth time, let it slap down again on the vinyl, and snorted. 'Better do what I'm doing, then.'

Fabien sighed.

She swung round on him, hands prickling from the dirty water. 'You're not waiting for me to do your cleaning for you, are you? *Are you?*' She watched a tell-tale flush creep up his face even while he stammered a denial, and felt anger stain her own cheeks. 'Well, you can either roll up your sleeves and get on with it yourself, or you can jolly well live in the muck, because being your cleaner *is not* what I came to France for!'

After a decent night's sleep, Briony woke in a more positive mood to a gleam of sunlight through the window and a room that now smelt more of frequent-wash lemon shampoo than musty dust. She was dismayed, however, when she clattered downstairs in her work jeans, to find that Honoriane had earmarked her to serve breakfast.

'Oh,' she said, when Honoriane directed her to begin slicing crusty bread and lay it out on thick plates on the large table with the steaming, milky coffee. Fabien and a very taciturn Marius took their seats alongside Honoriane, and two brown chickens stalked in on pink feet to settle beneath the table.

Briony was obliged to jump up throughout breakfast, making and pouring fresh coffee, slicing bread and locating more yellow butter in the big old refrigerator, scarcely finding time to eat her own meal in between.

Slowly, it dawned on her that the role Honoriane envisaged for Briony was a domestic one. Her heart slumped heavily. Hoeing and weeding hadn't been that inspiring, but being cooped up in a kitchen, a gloomy, dismal one at that, was still less desirable.

At lunch – more bread but with cheese and soup full of vegetables – Briony left everyone else around the kitchen table and carried her food defiantly out into the sunshine, settling on a hay bale and keeping a careful eye on her bread and cheese whilst she spooned up her soup, ready to drive the beady-eyed hens away if they thought to help themselves. She was blessed if she was going to be bullied by chickens.

The soup and the coffee were both delicious. The cheese was strong, but she ate it anyway, she was hungry after a morning of washing up, peeling and slicing vegetables for the soup, then cleaning and chopping a mountain of plums to go into an enormous jam pan for Honoriane to tend.

Honoriane, a tall, drab, almost silent woman, had conquered the language barrier by demonstrating Briony's tasks with dumb-show, peeling and chopping a carrot and then pressing the handle of the knife and another carrot into Briony's hands and saying, softly, just one word, '*Vite!*' Quick! She wasn't unkind, but she certainly wasn't interested in being friends.

Presently, Fabien came out into the sun to share her hay bale and drink his coffee. 'Okay?'

Briony shrugged.

He slid an arm around her and kissed her hair, just above her ear. 'Not okay?'

'I don't like it here,' she said, bluntly, shifting herself out of his embrace and swivelling to face him. She switched to German, the language they could both speak well, to ensure he'd understand. 'I don't feel welcome, I don't think Marius has addressed a single word to me. And I'd assumed I'd be working outside, like you, as I did at Tante Rose's. I didn't bargain for being cooped up in a kitchen, peeling vegetables and serving other people their coffee. Nor did I expect the house to be so neglected, so seldom cleaned – or have chickens under the chairs! What next? Pigs in the beds? It's *grausig.*' She used the nearest word she could think of to 'grotty'.

Fab took her hands, smiling. 'Marius doesn't keep pigs. It will have to be turkeys.' He made a comical face at the large pen of babbling black turkeys, which Briony had seated herself well away from.

Briony repossessed her hands. It was all right for Fab to joke, but to her it was no laughing matter. Apart from their board and lodgings they were being paid a pittance, which would have been okay if she'd felt they were being treated fairly, and if their lodgings were half-way pleasant.

'Time to return to the kitchen,' she said shortly, picking up her dishes and leaving him sitting on the prickly bale.

'It's honest work, to work in a house,' he called after her on a note of annoyance.

'I'm sure it is,' she tossed back, 'but it's not the work for me!'

But she stuck it out for a week.

She learnt how to knead bread and mix cakes, she washed and ironed and carried wood for the range, she peeled and chopped things for the gurgling pans and enormous casseroles Honoriane tended, she made coffee for the men and carried it out to where they worked in rows of vegetables. She was a *boniche*, a maid.

To stave off the aching tedium she wore her personal stereo until she'd used up all her batteries and was fed-up of her discs. The only bright spot in the day was feeding the turkeys, when she laughed to see them galloping up to her with spread black wings and wide-mouthed, voracious greed.

'I don't think I can put up with this much longer,' she confessed to Fabien.

Her boyfriend shrugged apologetically. 'But I've told Marius and Honoriane we will work for a season.' 'Season' seemed to be an elastic term that seemed to mean 'as long as they want us'.

'I want to leave.'

Fabien put his arm around her. 'But we have here a place.'

Briony gripped his hand tightly. 'But it's a place I hate,' she said, vehemently. Fabien put both arms around her and tried to console her with kisses.

Next day, instead of beginning work in the kitchen after breakfast, Briony returned to her barely bearable room and packed her jaunty red suitcases. Honoriane trod up the stairs after her, lifting an enquiring eyebrow when she saw what she was up to.

'*Je depart*,' Briony told her succinctly. '*Vite!*'

Honoriane plodded back down the stairs, and within minutes Fabien was racing up them. His face was red, his work clothes carrying a faint cloud of dust. 'You *leave?*'

Briony snapped shut the second of the cases. 'As I said.'

Fabien stared. 'To where? To what work? Is it that...' He began to trip over his English.

Briony rose, glanced around the room with disdain, shrugged into the backpack and picked up a suitcase in each hand, wincing at the weight. 'You can come, if you want, I'll wait for you to pack. But I'm not staying here. We can do a lot better.'

He looked uncertain, wiping his sweaty hair back from his forehead with a grubby forearm. 'Where do you go?'

'Back to Le Puy.' She made for the door-way, and he stood aside while she manoeuvred the cases to the head of the stairs.

'You have a job?'

'I'll find one.'

Fab looked troubled. 'But Honoriane and Marius, I say I work with them more long.'

She halted. 'Are you staying because you've made a commitment, or because you're frightened to step into the unknown?'

'I think two people in Le Puy without jobs is bad more than one,' he said stiffly.

She nodded, 'Okay,' feeling the sting of tears. Fabien was obviously prepared to continue in discomfort in order to take the safe option, rather than grasp his courage and make a change. 'You can leave a message at Nicole's, if you want to contact me.'

He followed her from the house, expostulating and entreating, finally growing angry. At the roadside, Briony put down both her cases, and kissed him briefly on the lips, then turned and began what, laden with heavy cases, would be a long walk to Retournac where she could get the train for Le Puy.

Back in England, through the kitchen window, Jim Reynolds watched his son, Guy, pull into the yard, hop from the cab of the yellow van, pause to fuss Ripple, the enormous, hairy but loving dog who'd recently foisted himself on them, then leap up the front steps of the bungalow between Dinah's petunia tubs.

'Done it!' Guy beamed, as he burst into the kitchen, brandishing a piece of paper. 'I'm a certified digger driver!'

'Well done, son,' Jim chimed into the chorus of approval.

Guy's wife, Sarah, paused, plate in hand, to offer a kiss. 'And there's pork pie to celebrate.'

Guy grinned and caught her at the waist. 'My favourite.'

The table was soon burdened with more of Guy's favourites, cold chicken, little sausages, potato salad. Jim settled himself in one of the carver chairs and noticed how all the foods that were considered bad for him had been placed at the other end of the table, the Cheddar cheese he loved, the pork pie. At his end were the salad and the skinless chicken with a few tempting slices of wholemeal bread.

He gazed down the table at all the things he couldn't have, and sighed.

Ellie, beside him, saw his longing scrutiny. 'Shall I pass you just a taste of cheese, Granddad?' she whispered.

He looked down at her conspiratorial little face and felt his own relax into a smile. He winked broadly, bearing in mind Dinah's remonstrations that he was trying to be too strict with the child and would be more use to her if they were friends. 'Just the tiniest taste, then Ellie. A bit of what you fancy...'

'...does you good!' she finished, passing him a sliver of the pale cheese, slightly crumbly, just the way he liked it.

Jim grinned at the half amused, half reproving glance his wife Dinah, tossed his way as he popped the morsel into his mouth. Then he began on the skinless chicken, lettuce and watercress. 'So,' he addressed Guy, between mouthfuls. 'We're getting a new sign over the gate, are we?'

Guy, with two slices of pork pie plus a lavish helping of cheese on his plate, ate industriously. 'White background with *J R Randle Contracting* in red and black. We're adopting a bit of a livery as well, I think image is important.'

Jim spread low-fat spread on his bread. 'Livery?'

'Oh nothing elaborate, livery's too grand a name, really. I've made up a template and I'm getting Tom to spray-paint *"JRR"* on each machine, hire tool and vehicle. It'll look professional.'

Jim snorted. 'Diggers get mucky, your fancy *"JRR"* will soon be obliterated by mud. Is this professional image you're after responsible for you being so busy round the sheds with your paintbrush?' There was an edge to his voice, he could hear it, but he couldn't help it. It stung that all these decisions, small as some of them were, were being taken by someone else, and every change felt like a criticism of the way he'd done things.

He watched Guy lay down his fork and regard him thoughtfully. 'I'm doing a few running repairs, yes.' Their eyes locked a moment longer before Guy asked, softly, sympathetically, 'Difficult to give over the reins, is it, Dad?'

As he opened his mouth to retort, Jim found himself under the steady gaze of Dinah, and felt himself flushing. Her blue eyes told him that she sympathised, knew he was finding retirement even more difficult than he'd anticipated. But his health wouldn't allow for things to be otherwise.

It would just be easier if Guy would leave things as Jim had made them!

Guy watched Ellie and his father walk from

83

the yard, Ripple tugging a lead held fast in Ellie's hand, shaggy coat blowing in the wind. He was glad grandfather and granddaughter seemed to be getting along better, but could tell from the set of his father's shoulders that he was far from relaxed. He sighed. 'Dad's not finding it easy,' he observed, as he watched Jim and Ellie disappear around the hawthorn hedge.

His mother, Dinah, stacked flower-sprinkled plates and echoed his sigh. 'Are you surprised? This place has been his life for so many years. Try to be understanding.'

'Of course,' Guy agreed mechanically. 'But ... well, he did ask me to take over the business, Mum. If he wanted someone to do things his way, he should've employed a manager.' Running a small contractor's yard wasn't what he'd set out to do in life, but if he was going to do it, he was going to do it his own way.

Dinah carried a pile of dishes into the kitchen, Guy following with the tablecloth. 'I don't suppose you could put off your changes, while he acclimatises?'

It was Guy's turn to sigh. He felt rotten laying this further worry on his mother, but she was the one who understood Jim best. 'If I thought it would solve anything, I would,' he answered slowly. 'But I don't think it matters when the change occurs, it's the change itself he's resisting. And the property maintenance side of things is ... pressing.'

His mother turned away from her washing up sharply. 'Meaning?'

Guy hesitated, then decided not to hide the true picture. 'Rotting posts in the sheds, a leaking roof, a rotten window frame. Dilapidation. Things which Dad obviously hasn't had the energy to see to.' He paused, then added softly, 'And the operation looks tired and old-fashioned, Mum. Customers do expect more of an air of smartness, these days, even in a low-tech industry like this. I'm afraid if Dad wants someone who's just going to let things go to pot, he's picked the wrong man.'

Dinah returned to the waiting dishes. 'Well, Guy, you know you'll have to be direct, your father doesn't respond well to diplomatic hints. Pick your moment, but bear his feelings in mind.'

Later in the week, Guy thought he'd identified the ideal moment. The men who worked in the yard, Tom and Ron, had gathered with a couple of the digger drivers and Jim amid Dinah's flowers on the bungalow steps for a natter and a cuppa after work, and afterwards Jim came indoors bright and smiling from their company.

Guy found him in the lounge looking out over the tiny strip of back garden between the bungalow and the thick, iron fence that encompassed the compound. 'Got time for a chat?' he asked, easily.

His father's eyes glinted. 'All the time in the world, apparently.'

With a thousand things on his mind, Guy pressed on, disregarding the note of sarcasm in his father's voice about his present level of activity. With his mother's direction to 'be direct' fresh in his mind, he plunged in. 'Dad, I'm worried that me running the business isn't working for you. Would you rather put a manager in here, someone who'll do as he's told?'

Jim's smile faded. 'I can't see me putting a manager in here while you need a job! Are there too many things wrong with it for you to want the business?' he snapped.

Guy felt a chill settle around his heart. 'I certainly don't want it if you're only passing it on because I'm out of work!'

'Don't put words in my mouth!' Jim said shortly, pulling himself to his feet. 'I've passed the business on to you because the doctors tell me I shouldn't be running it myself! If you don't like it, don't do it!'

Sarah didn't enjoy 'an atmosphere', and there was certainly an uncomfortable one between Jim and Guy this evening. Guy's well-meant, but possibly clumsy, attempt to clear the air with Jim had achieved the opposite effect to the one he wanted. Jim's white head had been silent behind the daily paper ever since dinner. Sarah took the opportunity to let herself into the cramped office where she was going to be working.

She looked around with a sigh. Stacked ledgers, files teetering, drawers scarcely closing. Pauline, the part-time clerk who had just given up the job, had had her own ways of doing things. In the middle of it all, the pale grey computer lay silently in wait. She pulled her worst face at it.

Then she drew a chair and switched it on, waiting while it completed its clunking, whirring start up procedure and the screen lit up with a picture of soft and welcoming clouds, as if she could just fall into them and everything would be okay...

She lay her fingers tentatively on the keyboard. It had all looked fairly straightforward when the engineer installed the machine that afternoon and showed her how to make templates for the computerised books that were to replace the old, hand-written ones. Hopefully, she'd be able to make sense of her notes, and do it again.

After five minutes of clicking she felt pleased with herself, having succeeded in opening the right programme and even locating the correct file. The engineer had suggested she input the last month's written ledger on the squared tables called spread-sheets, as a starting point, so she began, gingerly across the columns, then gaining in confidence. Then, suddenly, the numbers stopped appearing in their little squares as she tapped.

Instead, as she pressed the number keys the exasperating, flickery little cursor hopped about the screen like a crazy flea, no matter how many times she put it back where she wanted it.

'Oh no!' she sighed. Then, groaned, 'Oh no!' And, 'Oh *what* are you doing, you *stupid* computer?'

A little chuckle from behind her made her swing round quickly, blinking back sudden hot moisture in her eyes, to see her youngest daughter, grinning.

'It's just your numerical lock,' Ellie said,

incomprehensibly. She reached over to tap a button on the keyboard. 'There. You must've knocked your numerical lock off by accident, which makes the numerical keypad function like cursor keys.'

Not really following this but panic subsiding, Sarah tapped cautiously at number 6. Miraculously, it appeared precisely where she wanted it in her screen document. She breathed again. 'Thank you, Ellie, I would've been here all night without that help!' She forced a smile, dismayed that she'd allowed a silly computer to upset her.

Ellie dragged up a seat. 'You looked like you were ready to chuck the whole thing through the window! Do you want to do a few more entries while I'm here? Then I can help if you have problems – spreadsheets drive you bananas if you don't understand the basics.'

Sarah turned back to her keyboard meekly. 'That would be kind.'

Two days later, Sarah received a visitor. Although Mrs Portenroy, dressed in jeans and a shirt, seemed a pleasant woman, Sarah wasn't pleased to meet her. Even less so when Ellie came through the gates after school, grinning all over her face as Ripple bounced on the spot with excitement.

'Hello, Ripple!' she beamed, throwing her arms around Ripple's furry neck.

The visitor corrected her absently. 'Actually, his name's Ernie.'

Sarah felt her heart nose-dive as her daughter stopped dead, an expression of horror flashing across her face. This was what Ellie had dreaded. What Sarah had dreaded it, too, while Ellie was still so unsettled and missing her old life so badly. Sarah held out her arm. 'This is Mrs Portenroy, Ellie,' she said in her gentlest voice. 'I'm afraid she's come to claim Ripple. They lost him last week.'

Ellie was frozen. Sarah bit her lip, hating to see her grief.

Then Dinah opened the front door of the bungalow. 'I'm just making a drink,' she said to Mrs Portenroy. 'Would you like to come in for a moment?'

Ellie sat frozen in her chair as everyone else enjoyed a drink and a biscuit while Mrs Portenroy talked about Ernie Ripple. 'He's Dad's dog, you see. Big, silly thing, isn't he? Dad took him in when he needed a home. Soft as muck, Dad is.' She sighed. 'So I said I'd come and get him, when the police told us where he was.'

Dinah offered Mrs Portenroy the plate of biscuits. 'I should think your father'll be glad to see him again?'

Mrs Portenroy took a pink wafer. 'I expect so. He loves animals, does Dad.' She munched her biscuit in silence for a moment, then added reflectively, 'Mind you, he'll see less of him now, because I've had to say I'll have him.'

Sarah abruptly peeled her gaze from her unhappy daughter's brimming eyes, and demanded, 'Why's that?'

'Dad's had to see that he can't look after a big, young dog like Ernie. He got away from Dad so easily.' Mrs Portenroy shrugged. 'Dad can't gallop along like Ernie can. I've enough on my plate really, with the kids and everything, but...' She shrugged.

Ellie stood up suddenly, screeching her chair back, her fists clenched very hard at her sides, her face red, her voice high and tight. 'Please,' she said urgently. 'Please may we keep him? We love him very much, and I'll take him to your dad for visits. I'll look after him really well, and not let him run away. Ever.'

Sarah held her breath as Mrs Portenroy looked a little shocked.

'Oh ... well, I don't know, I hadn't

thought.' But then a look that might've been relief crossed her face. 'Well, I suppose if Dad can't really look after him... Tell you what,' she decided, patting Ellie's arm. 'To be truthful, I need a great big lolloping horse of a dog in my little house like I need a hole in the head. Do you think you'd better ask your mum if it's all right?'

'Yes, it is!' said Sarah firmly. Anything to see Ellie's face light up with joy as she threw her arms around Ripple's hairy back.

Dinah looked up from her magazine. 'Hullo, darling! Had a good day at school?'

Ellie, her bag pulling her royal blue Clarke Connor Community College sweatshirt askew at the shoulder, shrugged. 'Do you know where Mum is, Gran?'

Dinah looked at her carefully. There was no sign left of yesterday's joy from officially becoming the owner of Ripple. 'In the office, I think.'

Ellie turned. Dinah heard her scuffing up the hallway, the sound of her bag being discarded halfway. That would have to be moved, it was the sort of thing Jim wouldn't be able to help making remark upon. He was making an effort to be more easy-going with Ellie, but it was difficult when he was struggling with his own problems.

'Mum...?' Dinah heard Ellie begin before the office door closed behind her. Dinah flicked over glossy pages, hearing Ellie's muffled voice, and then Sarah's. The words couldn't be distinguished, but Sarah's incredulous tone told its own story.

In moments Ellie was stumping off into her room.

Oh dear.

Dinah hesitated, then went and picked up Ellie's abandoned school bag and knocked on her door, which Ellie snatched open with a face of thunder.

'Just pop this in your cupboard, Ellie,' Dinah suggested gently. 'We don't want anyone tripping.'

Ellie took the bag, Dinah followed her into the room. She glanced at Ellie's lilac-coloured personal stereo lying on the bed. 'Listening to music?'

'No batteries,' Ellie responded briefly.

'I have; come into the kitchen.' Dinah drew her granddaughter out of the room, sitting her down with a fresh-baked cake and a drink of lemonade, before rootling through the drawer for her supply of batteries.

Then she sat down beside her. 'Now,' she said, as she put the cardboard pack in Ellie's hand. 'I think you're fed-up and upset, and I'd be pleased if you'd tell me why.'

Pushing her lemonade away, Ellie's glower gathered new force. 'I hate that school!' she blurted. 'And everyone in it! And I just asked Mum if I could go to boarding school, instead, and she said I was ridiculous!' Her beautiful eyes filled with tears as she wailed the timeless refrain of all children. 'It's not fair!'

Dinah smiled gently. 'Oh, Ellie, it never was! Children have always hated school and mums have never understood. It's difficult, isn't it? How about you and me have a little chat, and see if we can come up with something helpful? Come on, we'll take our Ripple for a walk. I don't think your parents would mind us having a few words in private.'

They set out along the lush verges, steering clear of the thistles and nettles which smelt sharp in their nostrils, turning off down a lane which ran between farm fields edged with ivy-covered trees. 'So,' Dinah prompted. 'Why's the school so horrible!'

Ellie heaved a great sigh. 'It's so *huge*, Gran. Everyone knows everyone, but me. And there are some girls!' She shuddered theatrically. 'They think they're so *clever*.'

'I know exactly the kind you mean.' Dinah nodded wisely. 'Let's think about the school, first. It's a lot bigger than your last school, is it?'

'*Huge!*' Ellie repeated, as if huge was a particularly awful thing for a school to be.

Dinah picked her way over a muddy bit of the path. They'd had heavy summer rainfall recently, which, goodness knows, they needed, but it had left all the paths churned. 'So you haven't learnt your way about? It's too huge for you even to begin?'

Ellie shrugged. 'I've learnt a bit, I suppose.' And then, honestly, 'I suppose I'll keep learning bits, won't I?'

'I'd think so. You're very quick that way. I can see why it's uncomfortable that the other children have all already made friends – and, of course, you've had to leave yours behind. Have you e-mailed them, in Germany?' She pulled up her collar against a sudden breeze.

'Mum said I could!'

'I know that, darling, I'm not complaining,' Dinah soothed. 'Perhaps you could show me how e-mail works, some time? Because I don't know.'

Ellie stopped dead in the path, just where the soil had been washing away from tree roots, leaving them shining dully underfoot. '*Don't* you?'

'Well, no, I just write to people, or phone,' Dinah said apologetically. 'It's the keeping in touch with is important, not the method.' She linked arms with Ellie. 'Now tell me about these girls, and how they upset you.'

Ellie dipped her head. 'They're just ... horrid.'

'Explain.' She squeezed the little arm wound round hers.

'They just make fun.'

'Such as?'

After another gusty sigh, Ellie put on a mocking voice. '"Here's Fräulein Ellie, the German sausage." Then they put on a stupid German accent and shout, "*Achtung!*" or "*Ja!*" And in German lessons they all laugh whenever I speak.' For an instant her lip quivered. 'And my German's much, much better than *theirs!*'

They paced along together, Ripple bounding about in front of them, poking his hairy chin out at the blustery breeze.

Dinah gave Ellie a moment to compose herself. 'I'm sorry, darling, but I'm afraid they're jealous. You've had opportunities they never had. You've lived abroad and learnt to speak a foreign language.'

96

Swinging Ripple's lead crossly at the long grass bending before the wind, Ellie said, 'Well, what do I do about it?'

Dinah squeezed her arm again. 'Can I tell you what you don't do, first? *Don't* get angry, and *don't* look at your shoes and go red, and *don't* tell them to shut up. That kind of reaction just makes them feel powerful. Do you see? Remain pleasant, interrupt them so they're not controlling the conversation. Say, "And how many places have you lived, apart from Northamptonshire?" Look interested, wait for their reply. Their jeering will begin to feel silly to them.

'If they speak in German, however badly, respond in German, nicely. Make it "cool" to be able to speak German. Offer to help people with their German homework.'

They called Ripple, and turned for home. 'I suppose I could,' Ellie acknowledged ungraciously. 'But some of them don't deserve it.'

'Children often act badly when they feel at a disadvantage. That's human nature. It's more productive to change the way they act then storming off or retaliating.'

'Maybe.'

They walked in silence for a while. Then, Dinah asked, 'Do you think your mum and dad have the money for a boarding school just now?'

Gazing sheepishly at the ground, Ellie swung Ripple's lead again so it made a noise like a propeller through the air. 'Are they very expensive?'

'Hugely,' Dinah laughed. 'And, of course, they won't want you to go away. They're already missing Briony like mad.'

'Briony!' Ellie snorted. 'Briony clears off to France and Mum's cross with *me!* And Granddad–' She stopped abruptly.

Dinah slid her arm across Ellie's shoulders. 'And Granddad thinks Briony's a little madam who's been allowed to get away with too much.'

Ellie shrugged, but grinned, reluctantly.

'Your grandfather, darling, is getting old. And it's difficult sometimes for someone older to remember that an eighteen-year-old is no longer a child. When your grandfather was eighteen, he asked me to marry him.'

'No!' Ellie's head jerked up as she suddenly entranced, eyes shining, lips parted.

'Oh yes! My father sent him off with a flea in his ear, told him to come back when he was twenty-one! Boy, was Granddad mad at him! He asked me again very next day, just to show my father that he couldn't be pushed around. It was a good job my mother had a bit of sense and got the two of them talking the matter out civilly, or I might've died an old maid.'

Ellie laughed and Ripple rushed up, panting through his unruly fur, as if he were laughing, too.

Once out of the lane, Ripple had to go back on the lead. Before they turned back into the yard, Dinah said, 'And try not to be too hard on your mum, darling. I don't think she's on top form at the moment.'

As they turned back through the big, black gates, Sarah was waiting for them in front of the bungalow, her face breaking into a great smile of relief as Ellie ran to her, calling, 'Shall I help you with the computer, Mum? We did loads of word processing at school today and I can show you some shortcuts!'

Dinah watched them together, Ellie chattering, the travails of the day apparently forgotten. Sarah nodded and smiling as she listened. She hoped it wouldn't be long before Ellie found friendship and affection outside of the family, too.

Two weeks after deserting Honoriane's

kitchen, Briony was at the train station waiting for Fabien to arrive from Retournac. She was immeasurably happier, both in her new position as au pair to two German boys, Jan-Michel and Pieter, who were benefiting from her English as well as her energy to play games and build tree houses, but also in her comfy new lodgings – the spare room belonging to Nicole's family.

Returning to a nice home after work each evening was such a relief, and Nicole's parents, Christiane and Alain, were lovely.

The train hissed to a halt. Briony's heart hopped to see Fabien suddenly striding down the platform, one of the first passengers off, his floppy, nutty hair bouncing as he hurried towards her. In an instant she was in his arms, all her dismay and disappointment over Honoriane and Marius forgotten. She beamed. 'You look all suntanned and healthy!'

'Because I am all day in the sun – working like a horse.' He pulled a face and she laughed as they set off for the café near the cathedral where they used to buy ice-cream from the man riding a tricycle with the cart in front.

At the café, big, flat cups of black coffee steaming before them, he held her hands. 'I should have come with you to Le Puy.'

She looked into his long-lashed, hazel eyes, and realised how much she'd missed him. 'Are you unhappy at Retournac?'

He brought her fingertips to his lips. 'Without you – of course. But, also, when you are unhappy, I should make you happy again.' He smiled. 'It's for me, to do that.'

She felt a bloom of joy. 'Next time, we'll handle things differently, stick together.'

Then he asked her about her new job, and she told him about Jan-Michel and Pieter and their busy parents who ran music shops.

But then a shout, 'Allo! Briony! Fabien!' And Nicole was upon them racing across *le place*, laughing, waving, and in a moment she and Fabien were planting kisses on each other's cheeks. 'Has she told you? There is a job and a home for you here in Le Puy!'

Fabien looked at Briony in amazement. 'Is this true?'

She shrugged. 'Ye-es...' She wished Nicole had left it to her to broach the subject. She wasn't sure, despite his earlier words, that he was ready to leave Marius without completing his 'season'.

But his eyes had lit up at Nicole's words, so Briony plunged in. 'You remember Jean, who we used to meet here with Nicole and Claire? His parents take students, they have a room for you for a couple of months, if you want.'

'*Oui!* Yes, but of course!' Fab exulted, dropping Briony's hands to grab her shoulders and pop several enthusiastic kisses on her face. 'And the job? Do I work again on a fermette?'

Briony laughed at his enthusiasm. 'No, Fab, it's much easier work.' She hesitated, not knowing how he'd feel about the position. 'A job's come up with the dairy – selling ice-cream from the tricycle with the cart.'

She watched his smile fade from his face, and his jaw drop open. 'Is it that you make for me a joke?' he asked.

Briony shook her head, her heart sinking. 'No, it's not a joke. And it's a better job than you found for me – slaving for Honoriane!'

A silence. Then, slowly, amusement dawned in Fabien's eyes. He took Briony's hand. 'It is a good job, it is easy, as you say. I will be the man with the ice-cream. And I will be welcome each place I go!'

Chapter Four

Jim Randle lifted himself heavily from the car, and trudged across the yard to the house. Behind him he heard the swishing of tyres as his daughter-in-law turned the vehicle and drove it back through the gates.

Dinah followed calmly, waiting, without comment, when he turned on the top step to survey the yard, the digger and the two dumpers which weren't today out on contract and the tool hire shed where he could see two customers talking to Guy in the doorway. Dinah didn't chivvy or cluck, even though he was wheezing in the wind which blew between the sheds as if it were winter.

Instead, she took his hand, as if understanding his grief that he was having to let go of this business that he'd worked so hard to create.

He squeezed her hand, and led her indoors.

'Shall I make a cup of tea while you get changed?' Dinah whisked off her olive-green jacket. It had a pink ribbon pinned on the lapel. Dinah almost always displayed a pin in support of a charity.

He tried to cough, nod and smile all at once. The coughing won out, taking hold of him, snatching his breath. He felt an ominous tightness in the centre of his chest. A too-familiar heaviness set in, and he was aware of Dinah's frown.

Once in the comfortable bedroom they shared, he extracted a small bottle from his pocket, popped out a pill and slipped it under his tongue, then let himself roll down onto the bed for five minutes to wait for the weightiness to pass.

It was an hour later when he realised with a start that there was a subdued confab in progress at his door. He must've fallen asleep. His head felt hot and achy, but the weight in his chest had eased. He could hear Dinah's whisper. 'The doctor says it's a chest infection brought on by that flu he had.'

Then Guy, their son. 'He must feel rotten to be lying down like this in the middle of the day. Most unlike Dad.'

'Sarah's gone into town to fill his prescription for antibiotics, so hopefully he'll begin to improve once he begins taking them.'

Jim joined in, with great dignity. 'I'm lying down because the doctor said to rest. And I didn't have flu, I had a cold.' Even if he didn't have flu, he decided, he was feeling heavy and tired, and bed was not a bad place to be.

'The doctor said it was flu,' Dinah reminded.

'Nonsense, I never get flu!' He winked at her, admiring the way her pretty silver hair never dropped untidily from its neat chignon, no matter what problems came to try her. 'Sarah's been a long time. I hope she's all right, she's been a bit peaky herself.'

Guy cocked an ear. 'I think the car's just drawn up.'

Sarah entered, face flushed from the breeze, cardigan huddled around her, a stiff white paper bag from the pharmacy in her hand. She came forward with a smile. 'Seems funny to see you in bed, Jim.'

'I'm only here because the doctor suggested it.' Jim took one of the capsules from Sarah's package.

'I'll get you a hot lemon with paracetamol,' Dinah offered, gently, 'and then I'll begin on the dinner. Come on, everyone, let's leave him in peace.'

Jim let his eyes close again, and his head

sank readily into the pillow. He really did feel rough, achy, weary and heavy-limbed, he'd be glad when this cold had passed and he could get back to normal. Hopefully, it was only the cold kicking off his angina that was making him feel quite so bad.

He hadn't really intended to nap again, but, gradually, found himself woken by a scraping from the bedside table beside him.

He hauled up his eyelids and focused with difficulty. Ripple, the oversized hairy dog Dinah and their granddaughter, Ellie, had adopted, had his snout pushed deep into a pretty yellow mug, and seemed to be enjoying, with much snuffling and jiggling of the cup, the dregs of whatever had been in there.

Jim groaned. 'You great big nuisance! That wasn't meant for you, was it?'

Ripple had to back up in order to extricate his nose. Once at liberty, he looked at Jim with shining eyes, licking his chops and wagging his tail. Then he fidgeted from paw-to-paw for a few moments, and sprang up onto the bed.

'Oy, get down!' Jim puffed.

But Ripple just turned himself in a circle and flopped heavily on Jim's legs with a groan of contentment.

'Ellie!' shouted Jim, glaring at the shaggy intruder. 'Ellie!' The effort sent him into a fit of coughing. By the time he'd conquered it, Ellie was trotting in through the door, her untidy, longish brown hair flopping around her face.

'Yes, Granddad? Oh, you've got Ripple!' as if that were a matter for congratulation.

'But I don't want him!' Jim grumbled. 'And he's scoffed the hot lemon drink Gran brought me.'

Ellie sniggered. 'Perhaps he's got a cold.'

Jim couldn't help grinning at the laughter on the pretty face of his granddaughter. 'Pah! That dog's got a coat like a polar bear. We could dump him in the North Pole and he wouldn't catch so much as a sniffle. How about you ask your Gran for a fresh drink for me?'

Ellie turned obediently, cup in one hand and Ripple's red collar in the other.

'Then you and Ripple can talk to me while I drink it,' he added. Dinah had criticised him for not being friendly enough with Ellie. Perhaps this would be a good time to change that.

Ellie was now used to the walk along the green lanes out of town to the bungalow beside the yard of *J R Randle Contracting*, and wandered home from school with a light step. The weather was still a bit cool for the time of year, there was even a suggestion of rain on the breeze. But she was free for the summer holidays!

The last couple of weeks at her new school hadn't been as bad as those that went before them. She'd taken her grandmother's advice about offering to help fellow students with their German homework, and it had begun a cautious type of communication.

Living in Germany for the past five years she'd acquired a grasp of the language which surpassed that of Mrs Wooding, the teacher. In fact, she was hard pressed, sometimes, not to correct the teacher's pronunciation.

At least the girls who'd once been uncomfortably vocal in her presence had ceased to refer to her as Fräulein Ellie, the German sausage. They called her Brain Box, now, instead. But it seemed a friendlier nickname, and they were apparently finding it funny to speak to her in German occasionally and allow her, with good humour, to correct their laborious attempts.

But still, it was brilliant to get away from the huge school for weeks on end. Even if she didn't have anyone to hang around with during the holidays.

Crossing the tarmac of the yard, she waved to her father and Tom, the mechanic, shaking their heads over one of the orange-coloured cement mixers for hire. Absently, Guy raised a hand in reply.

Ellie went indoors, dropping her bag and kicking off her clumpy black shoes just inside the door. She glanced around, surprised that Ripple hadn't come to greet her. Normally, if he wasn't in the yard with Guy, he came flying down the corridor the instant Ellie arrived, long tail beating, ears back, black eyes shining as he launched himself at her in a joyful bound.

The kitchen was empty – perhaps her grandmother had taken Ripple for a walk? She glanced in the office, but only Sarah, her mother, was there, frowning at the computer screen. Then she thought to peep in Granddad's room, where Granddad lay, unmoving beneath the quilt.

And there was Ripple, behaving as he did when he felt guilty, lying very flat on the rug, pressing his ears to his head and pretending he was invisible. The very tip of his tail quivered as she stared at him. Then slowly, as if he knew he'd have to face the music sooner or later, he sat up.

Ellie hissed, 'Oh, *Ripple!*'

In Ripple's beard, on his chest, on his paws, were stuck pieces of bright yellow sweets, tiny pieces of silver paper scattered among them. Granddad's cough sweets!

'He's a thief,' Jim's voice rumbled, from the bed. 'Your dog's stolen my cough drops.'

'Sorry,' whispered Ellie, apprehensive about Jim's reaction, because you never knew, with Granddad. But then she saw that his eyes were twinkling, and giggled in reply.

Jim pulled himself up on his pillows, and coughed. 'I didn't have the energy to clean him up, I'm afraid, so I left it to you. Had a good day?'

Ellie shrugged. 'Not bad. But I'm on holiday, now!'

He sighed, smoothing his grey hair. 'As I remember, the holidays were the best bit about school.'

Ellie laughed out loud. Ripple pranced to his feet, grinning doggily, and flung himself onto Jim's bed, tail whizzing round like a rotor.

Looking at him sternly, Jim wagged his finger. 'You're like a bloomin' earthquake, dog! Off! Your mistress can take you for a wash.'

She brightened. 'That's a good idea! Or, I wonder if he'd like a shower?'

'Shouldn't think so – so give him one,' Jim answered comfortably. 'Silly old mutt, he seems to have decided that as I'm in bed I must need company, and he doesn't wait for invitations.' But, Ellie noticed, Jim ruffled the young dog's hairy ears before guiding him off the bed.

Ellie spent a very entertaining half-hour trying to wash Ripple. He lolloped into the bathtub without too much resistance, but took a deep and personal dislike to the showerhead once the water was spraying from it.

'Stay!' Ellie giggled, trying to shove his big paws back inside the tub as he scrabbled to free himself from the hissing torment. 'Good dog, stay! Don't climb out! Urgh, don't *shake* yourself everywhere, you aggravating hound. I'm soaked now, look!'

Only half as bulky when his luxuriant wheaten coat was flattened by water, Ripple gazed at her with huge, beseeching brown eyes, tail tucked between his legs. He co-operated grudgingly while she shampooed him, picking off the bits of cough sweet as best she could, but turned into a writhing monster again the moment she turned the shower on. She was giggling and fighting to keep him from scrambling clear when her mother put her head around the door.

'Heavens, you'll have to clear up when you've finished,' she said, automatically. 'I'm popping into town to pick Gran up now, with the shopping. You can get Grand-dad a cup of tea when you've finished with Ripple, please.'

Once Ripple had been rinsed and rubbed with a towel, he chose to dry himself by galloping round and round the bungalow, rubbing his face on the carpet. Ellie wasn't sure what Dinah or Sarah would've said if they'd been there.

She put Ripple in the hall with a biscuit, and took Jim his tea.

'So,' Jim said, blowing to cool his drink. 'What are you going to do with yourself all holiday?'

Ellie shrugged. 'Don't know. Mum's asked me that already.' And she didn't actually have any ideas. But it wasn't her fault she didn't have any friends, was it?

She returned to the kitchen for her own drink, hot chocolate. The phone rang, and she answered in her most businesslike voice. '*J R Randle*... Oh, hello Briony!'

Her sister's clear tones sounded happy as

she bubbled about returning to Le Puy, and how nice it was to have made friends.

Ellie sighed. 'I haven't made any.'

Briony sounded shocked. 'What? Not one?'

'No. It's a huge school, and everyone's already formed groups. I don't like it,' she declared matter-of-factly, adding, candidly, 'None of us really like anything back here. It was much better in Germany.'

Dinner was over before Sarah got a minute to herself. She went into the bathroom and was pleased to see that Ellie had cleared up fairly well after Ripple's shower. She began running herself a deep, hot bath, feeling that she deserved half-an-hour to herself.

A few minutes later she climbed into the silky, bubbly water as if in a dream, and closed her eyes. She felt leaden and tired, and not particularly happy.

Was anything ever going to be the same again? Their lives had changed so much recently, Guy's job, her job, Ellie's school – she'd been mortified when Dinah had reported how upset Ellie really was over school. Why hadn't she noticed properly? Why hadn't Ellie come to her? Or Guy? Too busy, she supposed, and Ellie knew it.

Sometimes, she felt overwhelmed by the struggle to re-establish the family in England, and deeply missed their lovely home in Mikhlut with all the dark wood and old-fashioned carving. Her parents-in-law had been wonderful, so welcoming, but Sarah ached to be among her own things, in the family's own space, where they could be just them.

When she wandered back to the guest-room that she and Guy shared, well-wrapped in a dressing gown because she could hardly flit around in just a towel in Jim and Dinah's home, she found Guy stretched out on the bed, staring at the ceiling.

She sank down beside him. 'Guy, when do you think we'll be able to buy our own house?'

Guy shut his eyes, with a little groan. 'Darling, I'm sorry but I just have too much on my plate at the moment to even think about it. I have no spare mental or emotional capacity, all my energies are channelled into the business.'

Sarah swallowed her disappointment. 'I know how you feel. I often think my head will burst as I try and get to grips with the computer. Sometimes, I think I hate it.'

Guy laughed. 'But it's only a machine.'

Sarah bit back a sarcastic retort, because bickering wouldn't solve anything. But she'd just like to see him try and master the rotten 'machine'! Their new life had meant unpalatable changes for her just as much as for him. 'Perhaps it'll be better when I get a bit further into my computer literacy course,' she opted for, diplomatically. 'I went for the first session this morning. And did I tell you who I saw? It was Pauline, who used to work here! Her son's business is using computers, so she's got to learn to use one after all.'

Guy settled his head more comfortably on the pillow. 'That's ironic.'

'Yes, I told her I was having trouble under-standing how the accounts worked, and what was supposed to be entered where, and she's offered to come up and help me get to grips with it. Then maybe I'll be able to come up with the figures you need when you ask for them.'

'Good of her.' Guy's eyes closed.

Sarah relapsed into silence, losing herself in glum contemplation of spreadsheets and ledgers.

'You look very pale,' her husband said, suddenly, startling her because she'd thought him to be dozing off.

She nodded, with a sigh. 'I haven't been feeling on top form.'

'Probably it's the same bug Dad has.'

'It's not a bug.' She sucked in a deep breath. He had to know sometime, had a right to know. It might as well be now. She lay down, snuggling up to him, and took his hand gently. 'Guy, I'm pregnant. I've just taken a test.'

His eyes flew open, his brows came down. His dark eyes stared into hers for a long moment.

'That's all I need,' he said, tightly. 'Sleepless nights and another mouth to feed.'

Guy replaced the phone. Gazed at it for a moment. Then made his way slowly to his father's room.

Jim, who had a little more colour in his cheeks this morning, turned down the radio and patted an area of quilt beside him, indicating that his son take a seat. But it was Ripple who shouldered past Guy in the doorway and cantered joyfully over to answer the summons.

Jim looked at the dog severely. Ripple flattened himself ingratiatingly.

Guy waited for his father to shout at the animal, but, to his surprise, Jim just tutted something about 'careering around like a pony', and left the dog where he was. 'Something the matter?'

Guy wandered to the window, glancing out at the dark bulk of the sheds, the lone digger backed up to the fence, Tom busy with something on the floor of the yard. 'It's just Henerson's.' Henerson's was quite a big local builder, they used *J R Randle Contracting* regularly. 'They almost always contract just the plant, and use their own operator, but, today, they want an operator. And I haven't got one to send. They don't sound very sympathetic about it, I'm worried that if I let them down in this they'll transfer their allegiance elsewhere. I'll have to go myself.'

His father watched him closely. 'That's what you got yourself certified for.'

'But I've no experience.'

'They don't know that. You're a certified operator, you've got every right to go out on site.'

Guy nodded, slowly. 'Of course.' So why didn't he fancy it?

Once on the site, Guy felt like a fish out of water. Other machines rumbled around him busily, imprinting ribbed patterns into the red-clay soil with their huge wheels. The other operators seemed to make their machines move with fluid economy, blending their manoeuvres, frowning in concentration, making the huge machines almost dance around the job. In comparison, Guy felt slow and hesitant, and wondered whether the other drivers knew what a novice he was. He experienced a kind of homesickness for the large offices of *GB Schwarz,* the blue carpet, the black desks, the meetings, the sensation of being in his natural environment.

He was unprepared for the noise of a busy building site. Even with his ear-defenders clamped securely to his head it was difficult to concentrate, and he couldn't help worrying about what was going on back at the yard, whether Sarah was coping with the extra telephone calls whilst he was driving.

Anxieties bombarded his mind. Would the insurance consultant phone with the quotes he was waiting for? Insurance costs were rocketing at a frightening rate. And why did the VAT authorities have to pick now to decide that *J R Randle Contracting* was about due a routine visit? Sarah hadn't properly found her way around the books, yet.

Frustration rising inside him, he let the bucket on the digger catch the frame on the top of the tipper lorry, making the entire machine hop uneasily with the shock of it. He moved the digger back to the trench he was hewing out, ready for the drains to be laid.

It wasn't Sarah's fault that she wasn't confident about her new job, and tentative when he wanted information.

He was beginning to rue the day he'd put no fight up when Pauline wanted to leave. She's known her way around the books. She could've answered Guy's questions. And talked to the VAT officer.

As he operated the levers in front of him the bucket clawed into the red-brown soil again, jolting him in his seat. The arm rose, swung, dumped the load into the tipper lorry.

Poor Sarah. She was struggling in all kinds of ways.

His hands slowed on the controls. Running a small business was a hard row to hoe. In a large concern his job had had clearly defined parameters, he'd needed to concentrate only on what he knew, and was rarely asked to step into other areas. But now the buck stopped firmly with him in all areas, problems crowded him in a manner fit to send him bananas.

But he knew what was bothering him most, more than insurance quotes or VAT inspections or how smoothly he could operate the digger. It was that he'd made tears start in his wife's eyes last night, and he'd never done that before.

He could still hear his thoughtless words, 'That's all I need!' It'd been insensitive to concentrate only on the responsibility and worry a new baby might bring.

A sudden rush of shame stilled him, perched up on the hard seat of the roaring machine. He was going to be a father again, have his own child to hold, to love! He was privileged.

He thought of the anger in Sarah's eyes as she'd stuttered, 'I need support not blame! It's not going to be easy for me, carrying a baby a forty-three, on top of everything else! But, of course, the only problems are *Guy's* problems, aren't they? Only Guy's got any worries, only Guy's having a hard time. The rest of us inhabit a dream world, leaving all the stress to him!'

He pulled the digger arm in to its body, rested the bucket on the ground and turned the key to shut down the engine, climbing down from the cab to jump onto the churned earth that would cling heavily to his gumboots. He clumped towards the rest hut to use his mobile phone.

At the end of the day, he parked the digger in the compound alongside all the other diggers, bulldozers and dumpers, and drove back to the yard, going straight indoors without stopping to look around at what ought to be done. He carried a large bunch of creamy stargazer lilies.

He marched into the office, where Sarah was sorting through a filing cabinet drawer. She looked up as he burst in, her mouth an O of surprise.

He winced at the wariness that sprang into her eyes at the sight of him. 'I'm a complete idiot,' he declared, bluntly, putting the flowers gently into her hands and sliding his arms around her waist. 'Mum says she'll keep an eye on Ellie, I've booked a meal at eight o'clock in town so we can have a bit of time to ourselves.'

He lowered his voice, as no-one else in the family had yet been apprised of the news of an addition to the family. 'It'll give us an opportunity to discuss our new baby, and decide what kind of house of our own we can afford. Then we can ring around the estate agents tomorrow.' He brushed her lips with his. 'And you'll have to make an appointment to see the doctor soon, because we'll have to take very good care of you, won't we?'

He pulled her firmly into his arms, almost squashing the flowers.

Briony put down the phone slowly, after speaking to her sister, brow furrowed in thought. Her family was making her feel anxious.

She'd assumed that after the worry and shock of her father losing his job at *GB Schwarz* her parents and Ellie would simply fly home to England and establish a new life not too different to the old one. Guy would get a decent job that would afford a good lifestyle, Sarah would go on much as before, and Ellie would be found a nice little school somewhere.

Certainly, Briony had never envisaged quite how difficult and different their new life would be.

She could still hear Ellie's blunt summary of the family situation: 'Mum seems worn out and can't get on with the new computer, Dad hates doing Granddad's old job, and no-one except Gran noticed how much I hated the new school because everyone was too busy worrying about you!'

Briony had been so astonished that her voice had deserted her.

'Mind you,' Ellie had continued at her sister's silence, 'Granddad hasn't been so grumpy with me since he got ill, and he even lets Ripple get away with murder. He's poorly in bed so he can't come to the phone unless it's an emergency. It's not an emergency, is it? You'd better tell me again how everything is with you, because they'll all want to know when they come home. Hang on, I'll get a pen.'

Head whirling, Briony had managed to dictate the salient points of her new, im-proved lifestyle to her little sister before the call consumed all the euros on her phone card. To her surprise, she felt a pricking at the back of her eyes as she said, 'I hope you get loads of nice friends soon, Ell.'

And at Ellie's stoical response. 'People are okay with me now, it's just that none of them are actually my friends. But I'll be all right on my own.'

Briony swallowed a huge lump, ended the call and pushed her way out of the kiosk. In the late afternoon sunlight, she set off to fetch her two charges, Jan-Michel and Pieter, from their piano practice, and take

123

them home for a meal before her employers returned from work.

The boys were loud and boisterous, as they always were after being kept captive at the piano for an hour, and she talked to them calmly in German until they settled down to walk more sensibly by her side. Then she began to make her shorter, simpler sentences English, so that they could carry the sense of the conversation comfortably in their heads as they practised their English conversation.

But what they saw as they passed through the town, they possessed the correct vocabulary for in several languages. *'Eis!* Ice-cream! *La glace!'*

And there came Fabien, pedalling up the hill on his large tricycle attached to the brightly-decorated ice-cream cart at the front, a back-pack on his back and a leather money-wallet at his waist.

'They're glad to see you,' Briony joked, taking out her purse whilst the boys made their selections. Helmut, the boys' father, furnished her with a small daily allowance to provide his sons with little treats such as this.

Jan-Michel and Pieter retired to a nearby wall to enjoy their ices, arguing the merits of chocolate ice cream and strawberry.

'You finish your work soon?' enquired Fabien. His hair blew in the wind as he stood beside the tricycle, self-consciously propping his hands on the red plastic grips of the handlebars with red ribbons streaming out from each end.

'In an hour or two, after *le dejeuner* for the children.'

He sighed. 'I now begin my evening tour. It will be long before I end.' There was no smile in his eyes.

'I won't be offended if you give the job up,' Briony pointed out calmly. She suspected that Fab felt being an ice-cream man on a tricycle was beneath his dignity.

He sighed again. 'And where do I go?'

'Wherever you want! It's up to you to ask around, and see what you fancy.' But she knew he was unlikely to do this, he'd rather remain in the job and complain about the evening hours and the toil of the hilly old town built on volcanic rock, than search out an alternative. Personally, she felt she wouldn't have minded the job. The hours were short, compared to hers.

Fabien liked someone to lead him, she'd come to realise more and more. Their first and second jobs had been courtesy of his

Uncle Ferdinand and Aunt Rose, both their present jobs had been found by Briony. He was not a natural go-getter. She found herself wondering sometimes if he'd abandoned medical school upon the realisation that he lacked the decisiveness and command doctors required.

'I'd better take the boys home,' she said, crisply. 'Because I've arranged to meet Nicole at *le Café Berac* near the medieval cathedral when I've finished. That's where I'll be when you've finished your job, if you want to see me.'

She took his small, lightweight back-pack, as she often did, because the straps became entangled with the money-belt and annoyed him, and she called to the boys. 'Jan-Michel! Pieter! Home for dinner.'

By the time Briony was ready to meet her friend, Nicole, she was worn out.

Helmut and Anna had been late back, they'd rushed in full of apologies and given Briony extra money, which was always welcome. But by the time Briony was able to hurry into *la place*, Nicole was tapping her toes and looking at her watch.

'I'm so sorry!' she gasped, throwing herself into a chair at the pavement table and tucking the bags safely between her feet. The tiny lights that snaked all around the tables were already flickering on in the descending twilight.

Nicole turned her dark eyes on her in mock reproof. 'Already I drink two cups of coffee! And Fabien has cycled here two times to locate you. He looks for his possessions, he complains you have his money.'

Briony laughed, ordering coffee from the table waiter. 'He gave me his bag to look after because it gets in his way. I suppose he wants to buy a drink or something and knows he mustn't borrow the dairy's takings.'

The coffee arrived, thick and pale and creamy. 'I think Fabien has not love for this job,' Nicole observed, picking up the sugar bowl.

Briony agreed. 'But it doesn't seem such a terrible job. And he should've stayed with Marius and Honoriane if he preferred the fermette. But in Le Puy he has a relatively easy job and nice lodgings, he should be happy. After all,' she took her turn with the brown crystals of sugar, 'we're living in his home country, which is relatively easy for him as everyone speaks his first language. I've never suggested to him that we go to the U.K, which I could easily have done.'

'You are wishing for home?'

Briony tasted the coffee, then sat back with a sigh of contentment, prepared to while the evening away pleasantly over coffee and perhaps a glass of wine when Fab finished his tour at about nine. 'A bit,' she admitted. 'Things aren't that easy for my family–'

But then screams and horrified shouts and the crashing of splintering wooden stalls cut off the rest of her sentence, making her jerk around in alarm.

'*Le voiture!*' screamed Nicole, leaping up.

And suddenly chairs were being over-turned as everyone sprang to their feet and raced from the path of a small white car racing directly towards them, bouncing over the kerbs as it hurtled down the incline.

Screaming, Briony followed everyone else, hurrying to get clear of the out-of-control vehicle, tripping over, picking herself up, hurling chairs and tables from her path.

CRASH!

The car jolted up the pavement, smashing through the tables and chairs, and coming to rest with a screech of metal and broken glass.

Silence.

Shakily, blood trickling down his cheek,

the driver managed to force open the car door and stumble clear of the wreckage, clutching his forehead, gesticulating and shouting complaints and explanations about his brakes.

Briony turned shakily to Nicole, whose hand was clasped across her mouth in horror. 'A moment ago we were sitting right there! We were lucky we weren't–'

WHOOF!

Silencing Briony's words, a sheet of flame burst out along one side of the car and in a moment the vehicle was engulfed in a globe of fire. With murmurs of alarm the on-lookers backed rapidly up the street where they could watch the crackling inferno in safety.

It was there that Fabien found the young women some minutes later. He cast his arms around Briony. 'I saw fire! But no Briony, no Nicole!'

Briony returned his fierce hug, taking comfort from his relief. 'But our bags,' she whispered. 'I'd put our bags on the floor. My passport and my money!'

Fabien pulled away in horror. 'And mine! My passport, my Carte d'Identité, my euros! You left them there? We have noth-ing!'

For several long moments, Briony stared at him. Her voice sounded disappointed and cracked as she pointed out, 'I do have my life.'

Chapter Five

Sarah glared at the computer screen. She'd typed the names and addresses of *J R Randle Contracting* customers into lots of little boxes in the hope that with a couple of clicks they'd magically print onto individual labels. The addresses were in the boxes, the labels were in the printer, but transferring one to the other had defeated her.

Also, one box had changed into a column without her permission.

With a sigh she acknowledged that she wasn't concentrating. All afternoon she'd waited for Ellie to return from one of her long rambles with her overgrown shaggy-coated dog, Ripple.

Sarah and Guy had something to tell Ellie. Something which Ellie might not be thrilled to hear.

Of course, they'd also need to tell Guy's

parents, and Jim and Dinah had been so marvellous in giving them a home. But Sarah wanted Ellie to come first, she'd been too easily overlooked in the chaos caused by their precipitate move from Germany.

It had been a shock to realise that Ellie had confided her dislike of her new school in her grandmother, rather than Sarah.

Dinah had dealt with it perfectly, of course, being such a wise and thoughtful person, but Sarah was achingly aware that *she* should have been her daughter's confidante. She felt guilty to recall how Ellie had voiced a sad little request to be sent to boarding school, and instead of trying to delve into what lay behind it, Sarah, caught at a bad moment with the computer, had simply snorted that the whole idea was ridiculous.

Battling with her new job, worried about Guy and the business, Sarah had also been miserably anxious about her other daughter, Briony, and her unexpected decision to work in France with her boyfriend instead of returning with her family to England. To be blunt, Ellie was less trouble than Briony.

But that was no excuse, she scolded herself, rubbing at the small of her back. Barely into her teens, a new country, a new – unloved – school and the loss of her old friends had been a tragedy to Ellie every bit as enormous as the parting with Briony had been to Sarah and Guy. Girls of eighteen did leave home, of course, but Sarah thought then that it ought to be planned, discussed. Not just sprung in an almost offhand, casual, 'Well, I'm off now!' way, and scarcely a backward glance.

She looked at her watch. Then jumped at the banging of the front door – Ellie had never mastered the art of closing a door gently – and Ripple's claws clattering as he raced up and down the passage at the joy of being home.

Then Guy's deep voice, he'd obviously followed Ellie in from the yard. 'No, nothing's wrong, we just want to talk to you for five minutes. Let's see if we can find Mum.'

Immediately, Sarah jumped up and joined them in the hall, dropping an affectionate kiss on Ellie's cheek. 'I'll get the drinks.'

They gathered in Ellie's room as Dinah was in the kitchen and in the sitting room Jim nodded over the paper.

'What's up?' Ellie looked wary, and although she accepted her steaming mug of hot chocolate, she made no attempt to drink from it.

Sarah drew her to the bed, sat down beside her and pushed back a lock of Ellie's untidy hair. Her daughter was growing tall now, the pretty light brown eyes were level with her own. 'We just need to talk, darling.'

She hesitated, although she'd rehearsed this conversation throughout the wakeful night hours. 'It's probably going to be a bit of a shock,' she began, carefully. 'It was a bit of a shock to Dad and I. But I hope you'll be pleased when you've had a chance to get over the surprise.'

Ellie stared, waiting, eyes guarded.

Sarah swallowed. There had been enough changes in Ellie's life recently. How was she going to take this latest one? She exchanged looks with Guy, then took a deep breath. 'In a few months, Ellie, you're going to have a brother or a sister. I'm expecting another baby.'

Ellie's eyebrows shot up, she glanced rapidly between her parents. *'A baby?'*

Guy sat down at her other side and took her hand, his brown eyes were warm when they rested on his daughter. 'We didn't know it was going to happen,' he said, diplomatically, 'or we would've discussed it with you. It might take a while for you to get used to the idea, you've been the youngest for a long time, and … well, we thought we'd had all the family we were going to have. This has been a bit of a surprise.'

Sarah added. 'I didn't want to say anything until I'd seen a doctor.'

Ellie nodded, slowly. 'Is that where you went this morning?' She didn't smile.

'That's right.' Sarah sipped her drink, and watched her daughter's face anxiously. 'How do you feel about it?' she ventured.

'I don't know.' Ellie's expression was closed. She drained her mug. 'I think I'll take Ripple for a walk.'

'But you've only just come back!' objected Guy.

Sarah put one hand on his, squeezing warningly. 'All right, darling. And while you're gone we'll tell Gran and Granddad. Unless you'd like to be involved in that?'

She shook her head.

They went to the office window to watch Ellie stumping off across the yard, head down, hair shielding her from the world. Sarah sighed. 'I couldn't tell what she was thinking, could you?'

Guy shook his head. 'She didn't give much away. Well, in for a penny and all that – let's go and tell the folks.' He took her hand.

She made a face. 'I feel as if I'm a child

again, owning up to something naughty.'

And, for several minutes, that feeling persisted.

'*A baby?*' Jim exclaimed, dropping his newspaper in amazement. 'At your age? I expect it was a mistake, was it?'

Beside her, Sarah felt Guy flinch. 'A *surprise,*' she corrected, firmly. 'And a bit of a shock but now we're getting used to the idea...'

'We're delighted!' supplemented Guy, a note of warning in his voice. 'We're going to have another child to love, and you're going to have another grandchild. It means some changes in our lives, but we've had to do a lot of adapting, lately! We're looking for a house of our own.'

He grinned suddenly. '*And* I rang Pauline this morning and sounded her out about coming back to work for *J R Randle Contracting.* She and her son aren't finding working together the best thing for family harmony. She's getting on well on her computer literacy course, so she's interested.'

Sarah gazed at him in surprise.

He looked down at her, and she warmed at the light in his eye. 'We need to look after you, don't we? Plenty of rest, the doctor said, and I think you'll have enough to do with getting us moved into a new home. You don't like working in the office, anyway, do you?'

'Hate it!' she agreed cheerfully, reaching up to brush his lips with hers. 'You can't get Pauline back fast enough for me!'

And then suddenly Dinah was beside them. 'Congratulations!' she beamed, doling out hugs. 'A new baby! How exciting!'

'Oh! Um, yes, congratulations!' muttered Jim, belatedly, kissing Sarah's cheek and shaking his son's hand.

Sarah felt her eyes fill suddenly. With all the shock of realising that she was pregnant and then Guy's initial, negative response, she'd almost forgotten that congratulations were in order. A new baby. For the first time since doing the test, her heart lifted with pleasurable anticipation.

Watching through the kitchen window for Ellie to return through the tall, black, iron gates of the yard, Dinah wondered how her granddaughter had taken this latest bombshell.

Dinah had offered congratulations to Guy and Sarah because she was convinced it would be best if they saw this forthcoming event as happy, rather than unfortunate.

Who'd want to think of a baby growing up feeling its lot was to be sighed about rather than crooned over?

But, actually, she was hollow with anxiety. Sarah was over forty. Guy had just taken over a business that demanded long hours and produced its fair share of headaches. They had no home of their own. Briony's gallivanting was giving them sleepless nights and Ellie's distress in leaving her home and friends was all too apparent. It didn't seem an ideal time for a pregnancy. Too late, of course.

She blew her nose, then leant her head on the coolness of the glass. Oh dear, it was obviously her turn for the wretched flu bug that had laid Jim so low recently. Hot, cold and shivery all at once, her legs were beginning to feel like string.

'It is better that we go to Carnac, where is my home,' insisted Fabien, his face shuttered.

Briony stared. 'But we're settled here, at Le Puy. We have jobs.'

'Pah!' Fabien gave a shrug that was very French. 'I sell ice-cream, and you care for children. These are not jobs to cry over.' After a moment he moved closer, making an effort. 'I must make new documents, my Carte d'Identité, my passport and driving licence. Also, I have no money. All burns in the fire. It will be easier from my home, in Carnac.'

'I don't see why,' disagreed Briony. 'I need a new passport, too, but I'm sending for it from the British Embassy in Paris. I'm not going home to fetch it.'

'You have no way, there is no passport!' he pointed out. 'But, for me, it is more good if we depart to Carnac. We stay with my parents.'

Of course they couldn't sit at the café since it had been all but destroyed in the fire, and, anyway, they had a serious lack of funds, so they'd met on a bench instead, facing the cathedral steps where pilgrimages were begun. Briony studied him, noting the way he gazed at the medieval architecture instead of meeting her eyes. He seemed to be taking their problems very gloomily. A few months ago she would've suspected him of being heartsick at the thought of what might've happened if she and Nicole hadn't been able to dive from the path of the out-of-control car which, crashing in flames, had destroyed their bags and personal effects.

But it simply seemed to be that Fabien didn't rise very well to challenges. He wanted his problems solved for him.

And perhaps he was *homesick?* She considered for the first time that his parents were actually in the same country as he was, but still they hadn't met since last Christmas when he flew from Germany to spend the holiday season with them. She thought of her own parents, and that if she were working in Great Britain somewhere, no matter how far from Northamptonshire, they'd find each other.

She sighed. 'All right. I'll give notice to Helmut and Anna. I hope they can find someone else for Jan-Michel and Pieter.'

Fabien hugged her, smiling for the first time. 'You will like Carnac! There is the sea, and boats! It is a place of great history.'

Jim answered the phone quickly so as to disturb Dinah as little as possible. He'd peeked into the bedroom a few moments earlier and she'd appeared asleep, face as pale as the pillow beneath her cheek.

Having just recovered himself, he knew how debilitating the virus was. Although, he had to admit, lying in bed for a couple of weeks had helped break him of the habit of going out into the yard every day. He now found it much easier to take the hours of rest the doctor recommended, his angina had stabilised and consequently he was feeling better than he had for years.

'*Randle Contracting*,' he said into the receiver.

'Oh. Hello, Granddad.'

Jim's eyebrows shot up. His eldest granddaughter generally rang at weekends. 'Briony! It's nice to hear from you, but I'm afraid your parents aren't here, they've gone to look at houses with an estate agent. I'm on phone duty.'

'Oh.' Pause. 'So they'll be a while?'

'Back in time for supper, they said.'

'Oh,' for the third time. A small sigh. Another pause.

Jim had been around long enough to recognise an awkward silence when he heard one. 'Can I help?' he asked, gruffly.

'Is Gran…?'

'Laid up in bed, I'm afraid.' He listened to more silence. Tension seemed to crackle down the line at him. 'It seems rather wasteful to make an international phone call to say nothing, Briony! What's up?'

After another sigh, Briony spoke up. 'I've had some bad luck…' And the whole story came tumbling out, the car, the fire, the loss of her passport. 'I can send for a new passport from here, but I need my birth certificate. Could you ask Mum to mail it to me, please?'

He frowned. 'What? By ordinary post? What if it gets lost?'

'Perhaps it'll have to be registered or recorded, or something? I expect Mum will know,' she added, casually. 'But we're going to Carnac where Fab's parents are, so can you take down the address?'

While he scrabbled in the kitchen drawer for a pen, he thought hard. He didn't like this situation one bit and Jim, being Jim, was keen to see what he could do to change it. 'What money have you got?' he demanded, after he'd scribbled the address on the back of a phone directory.

Briony hesitated. 'I've got *some,* when I get my wages. And I'll get a new job as soon as I get to Carnac.'

'How much is the passport?'

Briony began to sound slightly resentful of this questioning. 'Eighty-five euros, a little bit over fifty pounds. It'll take about ten days by post.'

'How much will that leave you?'

He heard a sigh she probably thought

she'd stifled. 'Don't get too upset, Grand-dad, I'm fine.'

'Except,' he said, dryly, 'that you're stuck in another country with almost no money, no job, no passport, and you're going to cast yourself upon the charity of people you've never met?'

A tense, bristling silence. Then, 'That's about the size of it, I suppose.'

'So, that's about the size of it,' Jim said gently. It was late in the afternoon and the sitting room at the back of the bungalow was flooded with evening sunshine. Too late to do much about Briony's problem, but he'd opted to tell her parents face-to-face rather than alert them by mobile phone.

He looked from Guy's stunned expression to Sarah's horrified one. 'She's in a bit of a jam. The main thing is that she got away without injury, but it's important to organise a new passport, obviously. Good thing she can stay with her boyfriend's people for a week or two while she gets back on her feet financially.'

Jim was well aware that he was putting a wildly different spin on things for the benefit of his son and daughter-in-law than he had earlier for his granddaughter. He'd apologised to Briony for being so hard on her, but he thought it was important for her to see what a potentially awkward spot she was in. All the money she'd had in the world had been destroyed. This Fabien had a French bank account, naturally, but, equally naturally, it was almost empty. It seemed to Jim that Briony was one step from being destitute.

'Her birth certificate's with all the other family documents,' Sarah managed, eventually. She looked almost as ashen as Dinah, who still tossed restlessly in her bed. 'I'll find out the safest way to send it. Do you think it'll arrive safely? Oh dear!' Her eyes filled with tears. 'Poor Briony! She must've been distraught!'

Guy slid a comforting arm around her. 'We'll have to send some money, we can't have her scrounging off Fabien's people. What's the best way of sending money abroad to someone who doesn't have a bank account in the country concerned? We'll have to find that out, too?'

'It's euros in France, now,' Jim put in helpfully.

Guy thrust his fingers through his hair. 'We've got a euro account from when we lived in Germany, but I don't know how to make that available to Briony!'

Guy and Sarah fell into worried discussion about the safest and quickest way of getting succour to their daughter. For several minutes, Jim listened to them fretting about ringing the bank and the post office as soon as they opened in the morning. Eventually, he interrupted. 'I have an idea which will simplify things.'

Guy and Sarah paused, frowns on their faces.

He smiled. 'Why don't I pop over to Carnac with the certificate and money, then you'll have no worries about things arriving safely?'

'Pop over?' expostulated Guy. 'It's miles, Dad! On the west coast of France somewhere, and you've got angina!'

Jim settled himself more comfortably in his chair. 'I know where Carnac is, your mother and I've holidayed in Carnac, and Quiberon, nearby. Just outside Carnac there's a site of prehistoric interest with thousands of stones standing in formation – you know how your mother loves anything like that! And my angina shouldn't bother me. I'm not that keen on nasty, cramped aeroplanes, I shall take a leisurely trip by train and boat. How difficult is it to sit on those? I'm the obvious person to go, aren't I?'

'I don't know, I feel it ought to be me,' mused Guy.

Jim nodded. 'Okay. It'll only be a few days, I'll take up the business reins again while you're gone.'

Guy sighed. 'But I'm up to my eyes, and you're not supposed to work those long hours.'

'And Sarah has to take care of herself with the new baby,' added Jim, smiling at his daughter-in-law who was fidgeting nervously with the combs in the side of her hair. Privately, he thought that she looked ready to faint. 'I'd be able to establish that Briony's really okay, and I'd quite enjoy a little jaunt to France. I'll set off in a couple of days, when Dinah's a bit better.'

Ellie was hot and fed-up in the waiting room at the surgery in town. She wished she'd been allowed to stay at the bungalow, or take Ripple for a walk around the edges of the fields filled with bright yellow oilseed. But with Gran poorly and Granddad involved with travel arrangements, her mum had decided that Ellie would be better with her.

Granddad had called Ripple a 'blooming woolly mammoth' that morning when the dog had tried to sleep on his feet. Ellie hoped Ripple wouldn't annoy him further while she was out. Or steal any more food. Or knock over any more ornaments.

The waiting room was full of woman in various stages of pregnancy.

All of them about half the age of her mother.

They kept glancing at Sarah as if wondering what she was doing there, but they didn't include her in their conversation and Sarah didn't try to join in.

They'd talked about the baby in the car. Ellie knew her mum was attempting to establish how Ellie felt about things, but she didn't really know, yet. She liked puppies and kittens, but they were animal babies.

Ellie looked at her watch. They'd been waiting ages.

Finally, the midwife in the bluebell-coloured uniform called Sarah's number. 'I'll only be ten minutes,' she said quietly. And Ellie was left on a grey vinyl chair.

She sighed and closed her eyes, wondering whether Ripple was getting bored waiting for her, prowling, click-click-click, up and down the hall, spoiling Granddad's nap. Granddad was setting off for France later in a couple of days. She wished he'd take her with him, she could pull his suitcase on its wheels and make sure he rested like the doctor said.

'Natalie! Catch hold of Liam will you, please? Liam, if you don't sit quietly there'll be no chocolate after tea for you. Olivia and Yvette, you share a chair, and I'll have little Isabel on my lap.'

Ellie opened her eyes to watch the woman and several children settle themselves. The eldest child, Natalie, she recognised from her registration group, a quiet girl who rarely drew attention to herself, and to whom Ellie had never spoken. Natalie caught Ellie's eye. Ellie prepared not to be recognised, but after a moment Natalie smiled. 'You're the brain box at German, aren't you?'

Ellie flushed. 'Because I lived in Germany. It's easy to learn a language when everyone speaks it.'

Natalie sighed. She had her deep brown hair in a tail high up on the back of her head, and flipped it with her hand as she spoke. 'Lucky you.' She paused to prevent Liam, a red-haired four-year-old boy with mischief in his eyes, from climbing into the plant pot of a sorry looking weeping fig. 'I've never been abroad.'

Ellie had been to at least ten countries, it

being so easy to drive from one to the other on the continent, but decided it was polite not to point this out. 'Is this your family?'

''Fraid so. All of them.' Natalie rolled her eyes. 'Liam! I said *don't!* And there's going to be another one – *don't Liam* – soon.' She nodded in the direction of her mother.

Ellie felt marginally better that hers wasn't the only older mum expecting again. 'Us, too,' she admitted. 'Mum's in with the midwife now.'

'Ahhhh, that's lovely!' Natalie beamed.

Ellie noticed Natalie's mum beaming, too. She smiled back, shyly. It seemed that some people thought the new baby was a nice thing. 'Do you like having lots of brothers and sisters?' she asked.

Natalie stared around her siblings as if considering the matter for the first time. 'I don't know. They're there, so…' She shrugged, and giggled. 'I suppose I have to put up with them! How many have you got?'

'Just one elder sister, until, you know.' Ellie indicated the midwife's quarters.

'When the new ones get born we might be able to take them out on walks together. Where do you live?'

With a bubble of pleasure in her chest, Ellie told her.

'Not far from us,' Natalie decided.

'I've got a dog, called Ripple,' Ellie blurted suddenly. 'I take him for walks all the time. Want to meet up tomorrow?'

'Sure. That'd be cool.'

They had to make the long journey from Le Puy to Carnac by bus, changing several times. Although they set off early the sun was soon beating through the windows and giving Briony a headache, particularly as her sunglasses had been destroyed along with everything else. The road rumbled constantly beneath them, the engine growled, and the loud chatter of the other passengers packed shoulder-to-shoulder thundered through her head.

At least Fabien seemed to have cheered up now he was going home, pushing his hair back off his face, smiling, and kissing her fingertips as he used to. 'Carnac is a good place,' he assured her several times.

Briony wondered why he hadn't returned all summer, if it was such a wonder.

At last, at the end of an endless day and after a final change at Quiberon, when the sun had become a ball of fire on the horizon and Briony was quite sure her head would burst if she didn't soon get away from its glare, they pulled into the centre of Carnac. Immediately, Fab began to shout in French through the window, then abandoned Briony and scampered up the centre aisle to beat the other passengers off the bus.

It was several minutes before Briony, obliged to queue to disembark, caught up with him. He was talking at a great rate to a couple on the pavement, and Briony even managed a smile to see how excited he was to introduce his parents, Luc and Giselle Vaux.

M. and Mme. Vaux were a very well dressed, spruce couple, and it was difficult to see any resemblance between Giselle and Uncle Ferdinand. Her life as the wife of the town pharmacist seemed a long way removed from his in baggy trousers and clumsy boots, hoeing and picking on the fermette near Le Puy-en-Velay.

They addressed her in rapid French, and Briony floundered to understand, and then formulate replies. Fabien had to help, sliding his arm around her and laughing.

The Vaux's house was set in a wide, pleasant street, within a rocky garden. Once inside the front door Giselle instructed her son to show Briony to a room at the back of the house, 'while we talk'. Briony caught that phrase all right, and tried hard not to feel slighted by being shoved out of sight so promptly. But at least, thank goodness, the room, however small, was clean and comfortable, its bedclothes and curtains dotted with delicate lilies, and she reminded herself not to be ungrateful.

She showered in a bathroom along the landing, then settled on the bed with a book she'd read already, waiting for the family conference apparently going on downstairs to be over. It seemed to take a long time. At least twice she was aware of raised voices. She would've blocked them out with her personal stereo, but had used up all the batteries on the bus.

Her head still thumped. She closed her eyes. And slept.

Fab woke her for the evening meal, fish in a thin sauce with potatoes and kale. While she'd 'had a rest', Luc seemed to have discovered the ability to speak English. Briony wasn't surprised at his proficiency, Carnac was, after all, a tourist area with not only the standing stones but also beautiful beaches and the yacht club. Luc ran a *pharmacie* where he'd obviously meet many British visitors. It just seemed odd that he'd persisted in addressing her in French earlier, although her laboured efforts to respond must've made it perfectly obvious that she lacked both vocabulary and fluency.

'I hope you enjoy your meal, and your room,' he remarked, slowly. He had a thick, black moustache, and it wiggled as he talked. 'Do you seek to return home, soon?'

Briony blinked. 'No. I'm living in France at the moment. Tomorrow I'll find a job.'

'You stay in Carnac?' he confirmed.

She stared at him. 'I don't know. We haven't decided what to do. Fabien wanted to come home to sort out his papers, or we would have stayed in Le Puy.'

Luc translated this for the benefit of Fab's mother. They exchanged looks.

Briony glanced at Fabien, who was paying close attention to his meal. It was a funny household, she felt, full of undercurrents. What she'd begun to understand, however, was that, for whatever reason, she wasn't completely welcome.

In the morning she offered to help Giselle wash the breakfast things, but was treated to a view of a gleaming dishwasher by way of reply. Fine. Briony trotted upstairs for her jacket and her last few euros. Fabien remained in bed, presumably, as she'd seen no sign of him, and Luc seemed already to have set out for work.

She bid the almost silent Giselle adieu, and set out for the centre. She discovered plenty of restaurants, of course, but she wanted to avoid catering work if possible, memories of Honoriane's kitchen fresh in her mind. She enquired about work at the yacht club but met with a decisive *non*. After a quick, admiring tour of the boats tied up to the shore, she strode down to the beach and found British tourists to talk to, feeling almost homesick at the sound of an English accent.

It seemed that many of the tourists were living in substantial campsites outside of town, and soon she was tramping on the verges to the closest of them. There she met a better response. After introducing herself at Reception and outlining her abilities, a tanned, elfin woman was called to talk to her. She introduced herself as Bernadette.

'We have here a club for the children, *Club Hilaire*,' she said, smiling. 'Always we have many English and many German children. Do you play games with children, and give to them their meals? It is an assistant such as this that we can use, a person kind and cheerful.'

'I can do that, I've been looking after two

German children in Le Puy,' Briony said, quickly.

It was arranged that she'd start the next day. The wages were low, but at least she'd be able to offer Luc and Giselle something towards her keep. She made her way back to their house with a light heart.

That evening they ate a kind of stew. The family members talked mainly amongst themselves, in French. She thought about addressing Fab in German to see how his parents liked being excluded, but realised that there was really nothing unreasonable in French people speaking French in France.

She went to bed early, pleading an early start next day as she was due at *Club Hilaire* to welcome the British and German-speaking children at nine in the morning.

Club Hilaire, she discovered, ought to have been called *Club Hilarious.* Under the direction of the large and jolly Hilaire they made wonderful pirate hats before staging a raucous game of swashbuckling on the high seas on the boat-shaped climbing frame on the grass behind the clubhouse. Lunch was taken in the shade, cheese and sliced meat and crusty bread with water and orange juice. And then the pirates were issued water pistols, and a shrieking, laughing water fight ensued.

By the time she'd walked back to the Vaux house Briony was tired as a puppy, but relieved to have once again landed a job she could enjoy.

She was surprised to be met at the door by Fab, a slightly ruffled looking Fab, whispering urgently, 'A visitor for you, in the *salon.*'

Wondering, she stepped into the cool room filled with heavy furniture, then let out a gasp. *'Granddad!'*

Her grandfather uncurled himself from a chair and rose, smiling broadly. 'Briony!' He put his arms out and suddenly she was in them, her face pressed against his blue shirt which smelt of Gran's soap powder. His voice rumbled in her ear. 'I decided to bring your birth certificate myself, and some money from your mum and dad.'

She pulled away from him to beam into his face, to kiss his warm cheek and pat his nearly white hair. 'I'm so glad to see you! What a lovely surprise, and just when everything was going wrong!' She pulled herself up sharply. 'Well, not everything, I've got a brilliant new job.'

'I thought we might go for a meal,' Granddad suggested. 'And your young man and his people, too.' Granddad was very courteous and correct, but the Vauxs graciously pleaded a prior engagement. Briony felt that Granddad had been snubbed.

But she had no time to worry about that! They found a lovely seafood café with striped tablecloths and she told Granddad her adventures in France, then demanded news of everyone at home. Jim asked Fabien a little about his plans for the future, questions that were, for the main, met with shrugs and non-committal replies.

At the end of a lovely meal Granddad asked Fabien if they might use the phone, as Briony's parents wished to speak to her. He was, of course, meticulous about paying for the call.

Briony dialled, pleased to have an extra call home to be able to reassure her parents and tell them how *cool* and *mega* it was that her grandfather had come all this way to bring her birth certificate in person.

It was when she ran out of breath that she realised her mother had some news of her own to impart. It began, 'Darling, this is going to be a bit of a shock. Dad and I were shocked at first, but now we're used to the idea...'

'Wow,' she gasped, as the baby news broke

over her like a shower of ice water. And, 'Amazing.' She talked to her father, as well, but was too stunned to do more than give one-word answers to his questions.

At the end of the call she replaced the phone and stared at it, numbly. Then, remembering he was there, she turned to her grandfather. She tried to smile, she really did, but somehow the smile turned upside-down and she felt her face crumple. In a moment Granddad's strong arms were around her. 'There, there, pet,' he crooned. 'There's no need to cry.'

'I feel as if they're replacing me!' she sobbed. 'Because I'm not at home!'

Jim clucked and pulled her more tightly against his chest. 'Your mum wouldn't replace you,' he soothed. 'I know Sarah, and it wouldn't matter if she had another nine babies, she would always love her Briony desperately, just as she always has, and just as she always will.'

'I know, I know,' she wept. But somehow she just couldn't stop crying.

Later, after Jim had gone to his hotel and the elder Vauxs had gone to bed, Briony made herself a cup of coffee in the kitchen.

Fabien sought her out. She hadn't told

him her mother's shocking news yet, she still felt weepy and empty about it and had to have more time to think, to adjust. It was silly to cry, *of course* her parents weren't trying to replace her, she knew that at the bottom of her heart. But still the idea kept revolving remorselessly in her head.

Fabien was unnaturally solemn and prowled around the kitchen with his hands jammed in his pockets. 'You enjoy the job, today?'

She nodded, hiding her face with her thick, matt brown coffee cup.

He blew out a sigh. Then said, in a rush, 'I think … I think in October I go back to *l'universite*. In Paris.'

Slowly, slowly, she let the cup come away from her mouth. 'University?' she repeated stupidly. 'I thought you'd decided that you'd had enough education for now?' Something inside her felt as if it'd turned to wood.

He shrugged, without meeting her eye. 'I have only one year left.'

She considered, managing to lift her cup to her lips and sip in silence. Then, quietly, 'So, you asked me to come here, you let me leave Le Puy where I was happy, where I had friends and a job I liked, knowing this.'

Fury rose to choke her and she switched

suddenly to German, to ensure he understood. 'I never asked you to leave university, it was you who told me that you weren't going back and that you wanted us to be together, work together, in France! You've *pretended* all summer, let me give up my university place, leave my family, leave my friends first in Germany and then in Le Puy, and all the time you *knew* you'd go back to school in the autumn.'

He lifted his hands in a fatalistic gesture. 'It is not true. I wanted an end to school. But my parents remind me. In France it is necessary that men serve in the Army. Medical students, they do not go until university is finished. If I do not go back to medical school, I go in the army. I cannot avoid.'

He tried to take her hand. 'It will be more good for me in the army if I am first a doctor.'

Trembling, Briony put down her cup. She was afraid that if she didn't, she would throw the hot liquid in Fabien Vaux's face. 'You'll never make a good doctor,' she spat. 'Doctors have to be trustworthy.'

Chapter Six

It was early in the day when Briony went with her grandfather to the station to see him off.

She hadn't been able to persuade him that he didn't need to dress formally to travel, and he looked unnecessarily trussed up in his cream shirt and brown-patterned tie. Taking the train to St Malo, ferry to Portsmouth, and then another train up the country, she was sure he could've made himself more comfy.

The station was busy with sighing, hissing trains and passengers who streamed past Briony and Granddad, some happy, some tired, some in a rush. Some to be met with beaming smiles and kisses on either cheek.

Briony watched a couple embrace, their eyes alive with love, their lips meeting with hunger. A kiss in a crowd, unembarrassed, unhurried. That was how she and Fab used to be.

She looked away.

'I don't suppose you fancy coming with me?'

Briony turned to her grandfather, forcing a smile. 'What? Without my luggage?' She tried to keep her voice light, understanding that Granddad was finding this leave-taking difficult.

Jim's dark gaze was suddenly hopeful. 'I could book in at the *pension* for another night to give you time to pack. We could leave tomorrow.'

Although she knew it would extinguish the spark she saw in Jim's eyes, Briony had to shake her head. 'Without a passport?'

Jim firmed his jaw. 'I'd stay for as long as it took if I thought you'd come with me when your passport arrived.' He waited. Then, 'But you're staying put, are you?'

She made herself ignore the disappointment in his voice. 'For now.'

Jim grasped Briony's hand. 'Briony, think hard about your situation. You don't have to stay with Fabien, you don't have to stay in France. I don't think that boy's been totally straight with you–'

'I know.' She squeezed his work-roughened fingers. 'Don't worry.'

After searching her face for several moments, Jim sighed. Then he delved into

161

his pocket and extracted his wallet. 'Here, I'd like to leave you some more money.'

Briony hid her hands in her pockets. 'Mum and Dad sent enough, thanks Granddad.' She felt like ending on an exaggerated sigh because Granddad would treat her as if she couldn't manage her own life. But she realised that his urge to help was borne only from love. An eighteen-year-old, to him, must seem little more than a child.

'But I'd like you to give Fabien's parents a contribution towards your keep,' he persisted, still delving about in the brown leather wallet.

Briony refused to be moved. 'Of course I will. Out of the money I earn – I get paid tomorrow. Look, your train's open for embarking passengers.'

Jim shoved his wallet away and glared. 'You're a cussed young woman, Briony Randle! You're going to struggle to keep yourself on the kind of wages paid by that holiday camp.'

'It's certainly a challenge, Granddad, but it's do-able.' Briony winked. She was pretty sure that Granddad wouldn't care for the solution to her troubles she intended, which was precisely why she wasn't sharing it with him.

His expression softened. 'At least promise that you'll do what's best for you, rather than what's best for Fabien. And think of your mum and dad, keep in touch with them. Remember that they love you very much, and they'll always be there when you need them.' Taking up the handle of his big black case he began to drift towards the waiting train, obliged to embark or miss it.

Briony swallowed hard and walked beside him as he headed for the gate. 'Thanks for coming to my rescue. Make sure you get a nap on the boat! Give everyone my love...'

Making her way home, trying not to think how much she was going to miss Jim and his gruff kindness, Briony mulled over everything that had happened since the Randles had been forced to leave Germany and she'd parted from the rest of the family to work her way around France with Fab.

Suddenly, instead of being a great adventure, her life seemed an exercise in going nowhere. Gone was the dream. No more peaceful smallholdings, rural towns, good country meals after long, physical days. Because, far from pursuing the simple, idyllic lifestyle he'd said he'd yearned for, *his* desire, *his* ideal, Fab was returning to precisely the life he'd led before.

She could see why he had to. What she couldn't see was why he'd made a fool of her by ever pretending it could be otherwise.

'I have no choice,' he'd pleaded over and over since the truth came out, 'I continue my studies or I join the army. It is the law in France.' And then, 'You can go to Paris, also, to find a job while I study. We are then near each other.'

But this offer had come far too late and felt too much the result of self-interest to sway Briony. Such a move would only change her locality, not her heart. Her heart had changed itself.

They walked a quiet stretch of beach that evening, the sea like glass in the still evening, its salt tang in the air, the sky purple and pink and clouds smearing the horizon in shades of lavender. Briony felt weighted with sadness and her bare feet seemed to drag in the sand.

What lay ahead? A job? University? France? England? If she went home to her family among the rolling green fields of Northamptonshire, would it be an admission of defeat? Her options buzzed around her brain until the only decision she felt able to make was not to make any. She'd made a big error of judgement over leaving her family to follow Fab, and she was intent on not making another.

'Fab, I need to talk to you.' They found a place to sit on powdery sand still warm from the day's sun. She watched the sparkling sea rippling onto the beach, and wondered how to begin. It seemed such a short time ago that she'd thought she'd spend the rest of her life with Fabien Vaux.

He reached for her hand. 'You are angry at me.'

She nodded, heart contracting at his sad eyes and the way his nut-coloured hair hung above. A sob rose, but she fastened her throat against it.

They sat, unspeaking, for a long time.

'I love you,' he tried.

Despite her best efforts, the tears started. She shook her head.

'Of course I love you!' His voice was urgent, angry.

She swallowed hard and forced words out. 'If you loved me, you would have put me first. You wouldn't have misled me, and you certainly wouldn't have dragged me here to Carnac when I was settled in Le Puy and you knew you wouldn't be staying here because you had to return to medical

165

school. Love isn't selfish, Fabien.'

The pink began to drain from the sky and the wavelets at the sea's edge sighed gently as the purple twilight settled around them. A beautiful spot for the ugly business of explaining that their relationship was over.

In the morning, Briony packed everything she had into her backpack and two red cases, before entering the dining room with its dark and formal furniture, to thank Luc and Giselle for their hospitality.

Luc wiped his morning coffee from his moustache with a green napkin, dark eyes big with surprise. 'You go home to England, today?' He shot a look at Fabien, who was occupying his seat at the table set for *le petit dejeuner*, but not eating. Giselle, presiding behind a chrome coffee-pot, frowned in bewilderment. Luc translated for her in a few quick words of French.

Briony shook her head. 'No. I still have my job at the holiday park, and Bernadette, my supervisor, has arranged for me to have staff accommodation.' It sounded pretty grand put like that. In fact, the 'staff accommo-dation' was one of a row of older tents pitched behind the office buildings for the use of casual workers. Briony would be sharing with Hélène, a slender, sallow girl who worked long hours in the camp coffee shop.

The holiday park was divided into two sections, the traditional part where guests pitched their own tent or caravan, and then the increasingly popular area where holiday-makers, on arrival, found a tent ready-pitched for them in its own little hedged area. Rather superior, these tents boasted 'all mod cons' in camping terms.

The staff tents were older versions of those set up for the tourists, but Briony's wasn't bad. Its blue and red canvas was a little faded, but it was pitched on level ground and even boasted a flexible board floor. There was water, electricity and a shower not far away. It would be okay for the few remaining summer weeks, although she knew her grandfather wouldn't think so if she'd confided her plan to him.

There would be quite an adjustment in her wages, of course, but it was still an economic way of living. Proper accommodation in the town would've required more money than she earned.

Luc's eyes returned to Fabien. 'I see there is a difficulty.' Fabien, although flushing, continued to study his plate without acknow-ledging that such a difficulty might have anything to do with him.

Lifting her chin, Briony agreed. 'There certainly is.'

Luc adopted a reproving expression. 'You understand, Fabien must finish his education.'

'Of course he must.' Then she couldn't resist adding, 'But he should have been truthful about it.'

Eyes narrowing, Luc seemed disinclined to comment further, and, after coming to an arrangement to collect her passport when it arrived, Briony went up for her cases. On the bedside table she carefully left the contribution to her keep that Granddad hadn't needed to insist upon. It made a hole in her resources, but she didn't want to feel beholden to the Vauxs.

'I'll leave you to have another look around,' the estate agent said with time-honoured estate agent magnanimity. 'Just shout if you've any questions.' He sat down at the breakfast bar in the kitchen and slipped some papers from his briefcase in a businesslike manner, his action almost obliging Guy and Sarah to take another tour of the house.

They climbed up to inspect the bedrooms again.

'It hasn't grown any since we looked at it five minutes earlier,' Sarah sighed. 'It's tiny.'

Guy hunched his shoulders and pulled a face. 'It's the ninth house we've looked at, and I'd say it's pretty typical of what we can expect for the money we have. And this one at least has the advantage of being unoccupied, so we wouldn't be stuck in a chain.'

Sarah pulled her hair away from her neck, she was becoming hot and sticky from the sunbeams dancing in through the large, uncurtained windows. The sun emphasised dusty smears on the glass. 'Even empty, the rooms are poky. We'd need a shoehorn to get everybody in.'

They took the few steps necessary to enter the next room, no bigger than the last and, in addition, featuring an awkward alcove. Guy rubbed his chin dubiously. 'I suppose we'd have this room and give Ellie the bigger one, putting Briony's bed in there in case she ever...' He didn't need to speak the final words *came home.* Sarah knew exactly what he was thinking. 'Then the baby will go in the small room.'

'Poor baby.' Sarah marched across the meagre landing to inspect the third bedroom. 'We had cupboards larger than that in Mikhlut!'

Guy laughed, his dark eyes crinkling at the corners as he hugged her. But then he glanced at his watch.

Accurately reading this gesture, Sarah went on towards the top of the stairs. 'You need to get back to the yard. Let's not waste any more time here. If we can't do better than this, it's a poor lookout.'

Driving home to where the town met the surrounding farm fields, Guy tried, carefully, 'I don't know that we are going to be able to do better than that house, you know.' He felt Sarah tense beside him.

Her voice wavered when she answered. 'I don't totally understand how we've ended up in such a weak position. We owned a house in England before we went to Germany. We sold it. It was a lovely big house, we should've had funds to come back to!'

'Unfortunately, it had a lovely big mortgage, too.' Guy sighed, checked his mirrors and pulled over, switching off the ignition. He turned to Sarah. She was pale, he saw. So often, these days, she was. She never complained – or hardly ever – but he was aware of how desperately she missed their old life, her friend, Marika, the beautiful village looking out over fields of sunflowers and marching pine woods.

How he wished he could just wave a wand and put everything right for her. If only life were so simple! He touched a lock of her long, fair hair where it lay on her shoulders. 'We could afford a big mortgage because I earned a big salary. What we got to invest was what was left after paying back the mortgage, plus expenses. It seemed a good amount, but while we've been away investments have performed very poorly, while the price of property has escalated. In those five years we rather got left behind.'

Sarah reached up and stroked his face. Her fingertips were chill on his skin and he caught her hand in his to warm it. 'Can't the business pay you any more than it does? Your dad seemed to make a good living from it. Look at the size of the bungalow!'

Guy kissed her palm. 'Dad made his money years ago. Paid the mortgage off years ago, when things were different. And he suffered no big financial setback.' He hesitated. 'If anything, I'd like to see money going *into* the business, not being taken out. The property must be worth a bob or two, but our overheads like insurance and health and safety requirements are accelerating at such a rate there's never anything left over

171

for the upkeep of the sheds or new tool hire equipment. Trouble is, both are essential. I need to talk it over with Dad. He'll be too tired when he gets home from France tonight, but it'll have to be raised soon.'

He pulled her gently into his arms, making his voice soft and sympathetic. 'I think we're going to have to consider this house seriously. It's small, but it might be the best we can do.'

Sighing, Sarah rested her head on his shoulder. After a minute she replied, 'I can see a horrible problem looming. Small house – big dog. And, to complicate things, a new baby.'

Silence. Guy shut his eyes slowly, and groaned. 'Oh no! You're right. Why does it always seem to be Ellie who suffers? Poor kid. I don't think I can face telling her we've got to find new owners for her dog. I wonder whether Mum and Dad will let Ripple live at the yard, with them?'

Dinah was feeling better.

Not better as in cured, but definitely as in improved. At least she felt able to face getting dressed to welcome Jim home, and to join the family at the table for a late supper. 'This looks delicious.' She smiled at Sarah, who'd prepared the meal.

'Lovely to be back to home-cooking. Smashing.' Jim took up his knife and fork from the red-check tablecloth with an air of anticipation as Sarah spooned new potatoes onto his plate.

Her own appetite diminished by the flu virus, Dinah pecked and picked at a tiny portion and had plenty of opportunity to observe Jim. She'd been horrified when he'd elected to take Briony's birth certificate to her rather than commit it to the vagaries of the international postal system, but, although he looked tired and a little drawn he'd evidently survived his 'jaunt' across to the west coast of France without ill effects.

Thankfully, Sarah and Guy were managing to refrain from bombarding him with questions as he worked his way through his meal. No matter how greedy they were for news, he'd had a long journey and deserved to eat his supper in peace.

'Well, I found young Briony in good health,' he began eventually, sitting back, pushing away his empty plate, gaining everyone's immediate and rapt attention. 'Fabien's parents live in a nice house in a nice area, and they'd let her have a comfy room. They've got it painted white, the house, in a big garden with a wall round.'

The expected bombardment began. 'Is Briony happy?' demanded Sarah.

'Did we send enough money?'

'Are things still the same between her and Fabien?'

'Did she say what they're going to do next? Will she stay in France much longer?'

Sarah pounced on that. 'We could visit her, too, couldn't we, Guy? Perhaps she could find us a cheap B&B.'

Jim waited patiently for them to settle down, and then told them all he knew. When he got to the 'difficulty' between Briony and her young man and his overlooking the fact that he'd have to return to university in the autumn, Guy and Sarah were shocked and dismayed into silence. Dinah felt for them. They'd suffered a whole lot of heartache when their daughter gadded off to France with Fabien, it was a pity if, after causing that much pain, the idyll was so quickly over.

'Was it all for nothing, then?' demanded Ellie, bluntly, staring around. 'All that fuss about *having* to be with Fab, even when it meant her being in another country, and all the time Fabien knew he wasn't going to stick it?'

Dinah, seeing Sarah's white face and glistening eyes, stepped in with a smile for her youngest granddaughter. 'Relationships are rarely straightforward, darling, sometimes people aren't, either. Problems arise unexpectedly. Perhaps Fabien wished he could drop out of medical school, and acted out a bit of a fantasy that he was able to. But I can see why Briony feels ... disappointed in him.'

Ellie reached out a hand to ruffle Ripple's wayward topknot. Her own hair, past her shoulders now, was wind-tossed from a long day outdoors with her new friend, Natalie. 'So why doesn't Briony just come home?'

Sarah pushed her chair back suddenly, and left the room.

Slowly, Guy rose and followed her.

Dinah sighed. 'She has to wait for her new passport for one thing, darling. Do you think you could carry the dishes out to the kitchen for me?'

While the young girl was so engaged, Dinah turned to her husband. *'Couldn't* you have brought her home?' she asked softly.

Jim shook his head, sadly. 'She's not ready yet. She's the most independent little soul. I'm quietly certain she is going to disengage herself from that young man. She just didn't want her granddad breathing down her neck while she did it!'

In their bedroom, their only haven while they lived at Guy's parents' house, Sarah cried softly in Guy's arms. 'Why doesn't she come home? You don't think it's because of the new baby, do you? Your dad said she was a bit upset...'

Guy's strong arms tightened. 'Of course not. She knows how much we love her.'

Although she eventually ran out of tears, Sarah remained in Guy's comforting embrace, his heart pattering against her. She reminded herself that whatever else happened she had Guy, she had Ellie, and Briony was more-or-less all right. Even if far away.

'What did Pauline want this afternoon? I saw her talking to you in the yard.'

She felt Guy tense immediately.

She sat up. 'What?'

He pulled a rueful face, his eyes concerned. 'I didn't want to tell you today, you've got enough on your mind. But Pauline's not coming back to work for us, after all. Her son's convinced her to carry on working for him. Her loyalties have torn in his direction.'

Pauline wasn't coming back? So she, Sarah, would have to continue to do the hated office work? For an instant, Sarah felt her face begin to crumple again. It wasn't fair. Nothing was fair. Life was so tough...

Then she wrenched her features firmly back into place. It taxed her strength to do it, but it wasn't *fair* to Guy to be so spineless. Every worry she had, Guy had, too.

So she squared her shoulders and even managed a joke. 'Oh no! I've got to carry on doing battle with that wretched computer, have I? Well you'd better glue it down – because otherwise I might hurl it through the window!'

'Why do the summer holidays shrink so quickly? There's hardly anything left of them.' Ellie sprawled in the long grass at the edge of a cornfield, eyes closed against the sun as she listened to the drone of bees in the cow parsley. The corn, recently a sea of gold, was now no more than spiky stubble. Beside her, Ripple panted, snapping whenever bees buzzed close to him.

She laced her fingers through his silky fur.

Something horrible had happened concerning Ripple. That morning, he'd leapt up to greet Gran and knocked her over, backwards, bump over the back doorstep and bang onto the concrete path that edged the lawn.

Granddad had been furious. He'd bellowed, 'That darned dog! Get him out of my sight!' while she scooped Dinah up tenderly. 'I'm all right,' Gran had protested, attempting to resist being ushered to a seat where she could recover. 'Don't shout at Ellie, Jim. Ripple was only excited, he didn't mean any harm.' But Granddad had continued to complain darkly all morning.

Ellie was trying to fill her mind with other things to forget about it.

Natalie, busy plaiting her long hair, grimaced as she agreed with her friend. 'Holidays always whizz by too fast.'

Still, Ellie thought, having to pull on her royal blue sweatshirt and return to Clarke Connor Community College wasn't the agonising prospect it once would've been, thanks to Natalie. A friend made all the difference to the lessons – and especially to the break times. And traversing the busy, noisy corridors. And the walk to and from school. And the weekends...

'Do you know when you move house?' Natalie broke off a long stem of couch grass and tickled Ellie's ear with it. 'We'll be able to walk most of the way to school together, when you do.'

Giggling, Ellie flicked Natalie's grass away.

'Geroff! I don't know what's going on. Mum and Dad keep looking at that house in St Anton Avenue. It's been weeks and *weeks* they've been muttering about it, and the estate agent keeps ringing up to see if they've decided to buy it. Dad thinks we ought to, Mum wrinkles her nose and looks in the paper, hoping to see something else.' She tore up a handful of grass and tossed it over Natalie's head.

'Pshaw! Puh!' Natalie gasped and spluttered as the blades flew in her face, and threw a handful back. It landed on Ripple, who snorted and leapt to his paws, barking loudly and racing in demented circles as the girls threw themselves into a grass fight. Ellie screamed in delighted protest as Natalie forced grass down her back, only breaking her friend's hold by tickling her savagely beneath the arms.

'I give in, I give in!' shrieked Natalie.

They lay in the beaten-down grass that marked where they'd played, as their breathing returned to normal. Ripple, after a few sneezes, collapsed against Ellie, making an already hot day hotter.

Ellie obligingly rubbed his ears. 'What do you think it'll be like when the new baby's born?' She squinted against the sun.

Natalie shrugged. 'It'll just make the family bigger.'

Ellie nodded, slowly. Natalie was the eldest of a large brood, she was used to the family expanding periodically. 'You like babies, don't you?'

'Mostly. Nice when they're not crying, better when they smile. Good fun when they're learning to crawl or walk.'

Feeling cheered by the reminder that babies were not just noisy inconveniences designed to divert a mother's attention from older children, Ellie slid one arm around Ripple, and the other around Natalie, and hoped that by the time she got home Granddad would've forgotten that Ripple was in disgrace.

'It's just come out of the blue.' Jim strode up and down the sitting room.

Guy stared at his father. 'What has?' He glanced Sarah's way, and she shrugged. Sarah's pregnancy was showing now. It quite suited her, she looked more relaxed, her hair shone and her skin was soft. He'd be happier if the frown lines would disappear from her brow, but...

Dinah folded her newspaper and lay it on her lap, her blue eyes following her husband's perambulations. 'Can you be a bit clearer, Jim? None of us seems to have the least idea what you're on about!'

'This damned cheek, that's what I'm on about!' Jim stumped over to the French doors and glared out at the lawn. They hadn't had much rain and the grass was more yellow than green.

Guy shook his head in confusion. '*What* cheek? Dad, for goodness sake, tell us what's going on!'

His father swung round. 'Mark O'Donahue! Do you know what he's done?' He halted suddenly. Put out a hand to steady himself. His breathing became shallow and rapid, the area around his lips suddenly bearing a trace of blue.

Guy went to him immediately. Jim was supposed to take life easy, avoiding fatigue and stress that might affect his angina. 'Sit down, Dad. Have you got your tablets?' Gently, he guided his father towards his armchair.

Grumbling under his breath, Jim took one of the capsules from its container and pushed it under his tongue with an air of irritation, then lay back in his chair.

Dinah rose and patted his hand. 'I'll make you some tea, darling.'

She dealt with everything with serenity and good sense, Guy thought, always knowing what to do to make things a little better rather than getting into a tizz and making everything worse. She hadn't even made a fuss at being bowled over by an outsized, hairy dog, this morning, which was very good of her. Ellie had been close to tears at Jim's loud anger over the incident.

Guy smiled at his mother as she passed. But he didn't miss the anxious frown that appeared as she left the room.

By the time Dinah returned with a tray of steaming mugs, Jim had calmed and was regaining his natural colour. 'Settled down now, darling?' was all she said, although she looked at him keenly.

Jim smiled at her in appreciation at the lack of fuss. He cradled his mug in a large, work-worn hand and went on with what he'd been saying. 'Mark O'Donahue, is the king-pin at *O'Donahue Plant & Contracting*, and he invited me out to lunch today.'

Guy nodded patiently. He already knew that much.

'And the reason he did that,' Jim paused, glancing round at them all with a ferocious scowl, 'was to ask if I'd be interested in selling him *J R Randle Contracting!* The cheek of the man!' He drew himself up. 'Thinks just because his firm's a lot bigger than mine he can stroll in and take over this company, and its contracts, and add it, a ready-made asset, to his. I told him he ought to call his business *Empire Plant and Contracting*, because that's what he's trying to do! Build a blessed empire!'

Guy studied him intently, thinking hard. 'Why did he make this offer? And was it a good one?'

Jim blew on his tea. 'Because he wants to expand, perhaps get some of the work where they're widening the motorway. There'll be good long contracts awarded, there. If he buys us he's got the expansion and removed some competition, all in one transaction.' He sipped from his mug, and then shrugged. 'It wasn't a bad offer, I suppose, money-wise.'

A pensive silence fell over the room. The sun had slunk behind inky clouds that were gathering as if for a summer storm, making the daylight sullen. Guy wondered whether Ellie and Ripple were far away, it looked as if they might get wet. From Ellie, it was only a small step for his mind to float to Briony, wishing that she were of an age where he could just open the front door and bellow for her to come in out of the rain.

His heart clenched. He yearned to see his daughter again, her dark curls, those laughing eyes. In a couple of weeks, if Sarah was up to it, they'd darned-well get themselves over to France to visit her. He'd have to make a window when things weren't so busy at the yard, and find the money somehow.

'So what did you tell Mark O'Donahue?' he enquired, absently, pretty sure he already knew the answer.

Snorting, Jim slapped his mug down onto its flowered coaster. 'I told him, "No thank you!"'

Slowly, tiredly, Guy let his head tip sideways, putting up his hand to support it. He was amazed to realise how much he wanted his father to have agreed to talk about the offer. 'You ought to look at the proposition from all angles before you dismiss it. That's just good business practice.'

Jim snorted again, his eyes bright with annoyance. 'I suppose you think I should sell? Put you out of a job and a home? Because O'Donahue wants the bungalow, too, you know, to use as offices. He's land-hungry, he's outgrowing his own place, he's young and ambitious.' He made it sound like youth and ambition were nasty diseases.

'I think you ought to at least *look* at the proposition, as Guy says.' Dinah's soft voice cut between the two men. 'And I think you ought to discuss it with us.'

'That's what I'm doing...'

Dinah laughed, her eyes alight, as they so often were, with amusement. 'Oh *Jim*, you're not! You're telling us what you've decided – that's not quite the same thing, darling.'

Shifting in his chair, Jim shot her a look under his brows. Glanced out into the garden. Looked back at his wife. 'Okay, then,' he responded, grudgingly. 'What do you think?'

Immediately, Dinah deferred to her son. 'Guy first. He's running the place, after all.'

Although this was the opportunity he'd been awaiting to voice all his worries, Guy felt almost too exhausted to reply. He wished he could just close his eyes and go to sleep here and now, leave all the aggro, all the arguing, all the decisions, to another day.

Instead, he made himself sit up and concentrate. 'I think we need to be very aware of a couple of things. One is that if you don't sell out to O'Donahue and he expands anyway, *J R Randle's* share of the cake, the contracting work in this part of the world, is going to decrease. He's bigger, he can supply more of what his customers want when they want it. Our profits might well fall, and catastrophically so.

'The other point is one I've been waiting to raise with you, Dad. I think money needs to be spent here. The sheds want a lot of expensive refurbishment, the tarmac's breaking up, most of the tool hire stock is on its last legs – Tom spends half his life resuscitating ancient old sanders and rotivators.'

'We can do the tarmac ourselves,' Jim began, bullish as ever when faced with a challenge.

'I know. We can do the sheds ourselves, too – in principle. If only we had thirty-six hours in every day! Or didn't need to sleep, or eat, or have lives outside the yard!

'So far as the bungalow goes, it really affects just you and Mum, because me and Sarah are already looking at houses. Although, I admit, we haven't found anything we're confident is large enough for a pony-sized dog and us.' He exchanged a look with Sarah. 'In fact, we were going to sound you out about whether Ripple could live here, but I realised that wasn't a good idea after Ripple knocked Mum over, this morning.'

'It was an accident,' protested Dinah.

'Yes, that was a worry,' Jim said at precisely the same time. Dinah raised her eyebrows at Jim, and Jim beetled his in response.

'But if you sold the bungalow with the yard then it wouldn't be an option, anyway.' Guy shelved that problem for the moment. 'Of course, I'd be back where I started a few months ago – looking for a job. But if O'Donahue's expansion adversely affects our business, I'll still be doing that, and the value of the business will have plummeted.'

Guy paused. He could hear the ticking of the clock on the mantel. He could never remember a time when that clock hadn't been there, tick-tock, tick-tock. As a child he used to think it was tutting at him when he'd been told off. The clock had been there all those years, all the time since it had been Jim and Dinah's turn to struggle with the mortgage to provide a family home.

'Of course,' he went on, 'this is your home. You probably hate the thought of moving.'

'You've lived here a long time,' supplemented Sarah, gently.

Jim's eyes were fierce as he glared at Guy, and his voice came out tight. 'Don't make this about whether we can bear to move from our bungalow! You've never really liked working in the yard, have you? Admit it, it's not like being a big cheese in a big enterprise with a big desk and a posh office. It's not like going to work every day in a swanky car and a crisp new suit!'

Guy gazed back at his father. Seeing the tiredness in his father's eyes, the rough hands, the body worn with years of working long hours, seven days a week. The anger that his son might be rejecting years of the same.

'No,' he answered honestly. And he had no idea that he was going to say the things he said next, until he was saying them. 'I don't much like it. I do hanker after my old job, our old life when we lived in Mikhlut in a beautiful house with our own things around us, when I had a job I liked in a field I was qualified in. And, if you were thinking of giving me a vote about it, I'd say sell *J R Randle*. Sell to O'Donahue, and let *him* worry about the dilapidated buildings and the capital-hungry stock, the insurance, the VAT, the tax bill. Let him pour his money into it. I'm very sorry, Dad, I'm grateful for the opportunity you gave me – but I've had enough. This job's not for me.'

And, quietly, Dinah added, 'And I think everyone realises that.'

Chapter Seven

Through the scratched plastic window of the shed that housed the equipment for hire, Guy watched his father, Jim, standing at the top of the bungalow steps beside tubs of still-flowering petunias, white and red. An incongruous note, a splash of prettiness in the hard landscape of the contractor's yard, flowers had been grown on that porch ever since Guy could remember.

Hands in pockets, mouth a thin line, white hair lifting in the early September breeze, Jim gazed around. *J R Randle Contracting*, his yard, his life's work.

A digger and two dump trucks not out on contract stood on the patchy tarmac, years of mud speckling their yellow paint and clinging to their mighty tyres. Beside the old black boards of the shed, Tom worked over a turf-cutting machine, his tool kit open, while Ron heaved a cement mixer onto a trailer behind the van.

Jim's eyes flicked from one to the other. These were men taken on by him, men he'd worked alongside.

Guy sighed. Jim, at the time when his health let him down, had been so deeply gratified at Guy taking over, working at the business that Jim had created, prolonging its life. Now Guy's conscience was heavy. It didn't matter how many times Sarah or his mother, Dinah, told him he was under no obligation to continue to labour at the helm, enduring the long hours and constant problem-solving.

Guy knew that by not wanting the business, he was hurting his father.

But it wasn't as if he hadn't tried!

There was no-one more aware than him that he needed a job to feed his family, the business had given his parents a good living in the past and it had seemed sensible to take up the reins when they were offered. But things had changed in recent years and the yard was getting less business, making less profit as competition from bigger contractors, and overheads, grew at a frightening rate.

And Guy hadn't anticipated how miserable he'd be to be tied to a job that simply was wrong for him. He'd begun to hate it.

So when Mark O'Donahue made Jim an offer for the yard to accommodate the planned expansion of *O'Donahue Plant & Contracting,* Guy just hadn't been able to keep his true feelings to himself. He could still hear his words, the relief echoing in his voice: 'Sell to O'Donahue!' And then see the shock-waves of dismay in Jim's face.

Guy knew his father felt let down, the yard had been his life and it was incomprehensible that his son found it a boring, expensive, labour intensive millstone.

Should Guy force himself to reconsider? Battle to get up each day and make the business work?

He hadn't had much joy in finding employment when they'd first come back from Germany, what made him think he'd be more successful this time? As the bungalow was to be sold with the yard, they could quite possibly end up without a home or a living? Would he then be stricken with yet more guilt at what he'd discarded?

Miserably, he began to turn away. But at that moment Dinah burst out of the bungalow behind Jim, her silvery voice high-pitched on the breeze. 'Guy? *Guy!*' Disregarding her years she ran for the steps, brows drawn down in anxiety.

Quickly, Guy ducked through the door to the yard. It wasn't like his mother to betray such obvious agitation. 'Here! What's up?'

She halted, blue eyes seeking his across the distance between them. 'Guy, the doctor's surgery's one the phone, they need to speak to you immediately!'

Sarah! Even before his mother had finished her sentence, Guy was running across the yard to the house, heart drumming. Although not due for a routine antenatal appointment that morning, Sarah had gone to the surgery because her hands and ankles had become puffy and swollen.

Conscious of his parents hurrying behind him, he dashed into the kitchen and snatched up the phone. 'Yes?'

'Ah, Mr Randle.' Dr Minton's voice was professionally calm. 'Try not to be alarmed, but I'd like the hospital to take a little look at Sarah. Not only because of the swelling she came to the surgery complaining of his morning, but also because her blood pressure has risen quite considerably. Now, potentially, what this indicates...'

The doctor's voice went on, kind, explaining, advising. And the moment he was off the phone, Guy was plucking his car keys from the rack on the wall, checking that he had his wallet, smoothing down his hair. 'I've got to go to the general hospital. Sarah's been sent in with high blood pressure. They need to monitor her.' He paused, turning to his mother. 'Can you keep an eye out for Ellie when she comes home this afternoon, and try not to let her worry? This is all she needed on her first day back at school!'

As he dashed out, he heard Jim call after him gruffly. 'Give her our love.'

Guy raised his voice to send it back, 'Of course!' even as he leapt into the car and made for the gates, forcing himself to drive sensibly and concentrate on the road, even though his heart was pounding and his legs felt watery with anxiety. The doctor had told him one or two things about expectant mothers with symptoms like Sarah's that had sent his own blood pressure soaring!

Sarah, darling, nothing must happen to you!

In the time it took him to battle the traffic and search out a parking space in front of the towering grey hospital buildings, Sarah had been admitted to the maternity unit. He found her lying in a cubicle in her white hospital gown, her hair swirling across the pillows.

And she looked very fed-up.

'I feel absolutely fine!' she began to protest the instant Guy pushed his way in through the yellow curtains, grey eyes stormy. 'But

I've got to lie here *all afternoon* while they monitor me, and probably stay in overnight, too.' She tutted in exasperation. 'As if I've nothing better to do than loaf around. But this swelling and high blood pressure can be an ominous combination, apparently.'

Reassured by his wife's robust vexation at having to do something so ludicrous as to lie abed during the daytime, Guy sank onto the edge of the lemon counterpane as he recovered his breath. His anxiety even began to seep away as he lifted her hand to his lips. 'It won't hurt you to rest for a few hours.'

She snorted. 'It's not going to get those letters typed, though, is it? And if Pauline's not coming back to do the office work after all, I can't afford to let it get on top of me, because I only half know what I'm doing in the first place! I wish that clever computer could do it alone.'

He stroked her hair back. 'Relax. The office will wait.'

She pulled a mock-horrified face. 'Yes, I know. It's *me* it'll be waiting for!'

He laughed, and kissed her soundly, almost weak with relief at finding her so much her normal self when every moment since the conversation with Dr Minton he'd suffered from visions of flashing blue lights and emergency procedures.

But, later, when Guy returned to the bungalow to pack an overnight case for Sarah, it was with the grim knowledge that his relief had been premature.

He pulled into the yard. The sun had sunk and there was a suggestion of twilight in the early evening. Tired and troubled, he rested for a moment, noting that two extra diggers had appeared in the yard. They hadn't been scheduled for return so either the hire contract had been cut short, or they'd suffered mechanical failure. Neither option good for *J R Randle,* and both depressingly regular occurrences.

Rousing himself as the door to the bungalow banged and Ellie and Ripple bounded up to the car, he managed to paste on a smile.

'Is Mum okay?' demanded Ellie through the open window, eyes huge with apprehension. 'Why's she in hospital? Is she ill? Why haven't you brought her home?'

Guy got out of the car to give his daughter a big, comforting hug, swinging her off her feet as if she was still a little girl, making Ripple prance and bark with delight. 'They're just watching her, sweetheart. They have to take good care of mothers-to-be. Especially older mums.'

And he pushed his own fears aside, slid his arm around his daughter and took her indoors to recount all the information he had, knowing Dinah and Jim would be just as anxious as Ellie.

'Unfortunately,' he said, smiling his appreciation at Dinah as she provided him with a hot cup of tea from a proper teapot, not like the lukewarm variety from the hospital vending machine. 'They're not at all happy with Sarah's blood pressure. It's risen very sharply. And with this swelling occurring almost overnight, they're watching her to make sure she isn't developing a thing called pre-eclampsia. That would be dangerous to both her and the baby, and would mean there's a problem with the placenta.' With Ellie listening, he chose not to spell out the possible consequences in detail. It had frightened him, and, judging by the expression in Sarah's eyes, her too. That was enough.

Three pairs of anxious eyes were fastened intently upon him.

'How is she in herself?' asked Dinah.

'So when's she coming home?' demanded Ellie.

And Jim, 'Will she soon be better?'

'She feels absolutely fine,' he assured them. 'Apart from cheesed off at being made to go to bed. They're going to keep her in until they're satisfied. And we won't know how long that'll be until we know what we're dealing with. They're giving her drugs to help bring the blood pressure down, and are quite hopeful that all she needs is rest.'

And he was going to make sure she got it. The doctor had been concerned about the stress level Sarah had exhibited, and Guy had had to admit that there had been a lot to worry about recently. This had caused the doctor, in his crisp white coat, to frown. 'I'm afraid that Sarah, especially as an older mum, will have to take things very easily over the remainder of her pregnancy. Ideally, she should have bags of rest and as little anxiety as can be managed.'

Guy had smiled grimly. 'I'll make sure that that's what she gets.' For one thing, he vowed silently, he refused to let Sarah struggle with the spectre of the *J R Randle* paperwork any more. The business could crumble to dust before he'd let anything happen to his wife and baby.

But now he smiled reassuringly at Ellie, who was still solemn and pinched. 'She's annoyed that she's missed hearing about your first day back at school, Ellie, so how about you helping me pack her bag, then coming back to the hospital for visiting time?'

'Cool!' Ellie's face cleared instantly. 'I know which bag she'll want!' And she dashed off to her parents' bedroom.

With a gentle hand on his arm, Dinah prevented him from following, concern and understanding in her blue eyes. 'How dangerous is it?'

He sighed, and patted his mother's hand. 'They're hopeful that it's *not* pre-eclampsia. But if it is...' His eyes closed on an instant of pain. 'The baby's not far enough along to survive.'

Briony finished her shift looking after and entertaining the children at *Club Hilaire*, tired from a mad game of tug-o-war, but smiling at the hilarity around her. It had been a hot day, and busy, even if the older children were returning to their schools now, leaving the campsite populated mainly by families with only pre-school children. What a hard-working children's club leader needed, she decided, was a cold drink and a nice long shower. Then perhaps a relaxing evening reading in the late sunshine, or chatting to her workmates... Her French language skills were coming on in great leaps, but girls of several different nationalities speaking it made for some entertaining conversations.

But as she rounded a glossy green laurel hedge and came almost within sight of her temporary home, she halted. A tall man was hovering outside Reception, which stood in front of the 'staff accommodation' – a row of faded red-and-blue tents for the casual workers – pushing back his floppy hazelnut hair and checking his watch.

'Fabien?' Her heart flopped. She tried to decide why this should be, and whether the sight of him brought trepidation or pleasure.

He swung around at the sound of her voice, and smiled. 'Briony.' A few long strides brought him to her, and, after a hesitation, he kissed her on both cheeks.

She flushed at the pressure of his once-familiar lips. Such awkward formality only emphasised how things had changed between them. Before she could decide whether she should return the salute, he stepped back.

'We can talk?' he asked. 'I have for you two things.'

'Of course. Let's go for a walk.' She

managed a tentative smile for him, and they set off together to the edge of the campsite and into one of the surrounding meadows, where long grass and yellow wild flowers flattened to cats paws in the breeze. It felt unsettling to be walking at his side. She'd only just begun to get used to being without him, and now here they were together again.

Fabien was slow to embark on the reasons for his visit, preferring first to ask after her and how she found living on the campsite, and to tell her in a low, urgent voice how much he missed her. And how could she respond? She'd missed him, too, but to admit it might give him unfounded hope of a reconciliation.

Eventually, he pulled out a flat brown envelope.

'My passport!' Briony fell on the package with a cry of glee, ripping it open and flipping over the pages of the little dark red book. 'Oh, thank you for bringing this to me!' But how like Fab to withhold the precious document until he'd finished saying what he'd wanted to say! Still, she thought, trying to be fair, perhaps he feared she wouldn't listen once the all-important passport was safely in her possession.

He took her hand to help her over a low

fence that she needed no help with. 'There is also a message, from your father. He ask you to telephone to your home.' He hesitated, his fingers closing more firmly over hers. 'I'm sorry, but when he telephones to our house, it is my father that responds. He tells to your father that you are not living in our home since two weeks. That you are living in a tent. Your father is annoyed.' He pulled an apologetic face.

Briony groaned. 'Serves me right for not ringing home and telling them I'd moved, I suppose.' She made to disengage her hand.

Fabien only clung harder. His eyes were soft, his tone gentle. 'You must phone to your home, Briony. Your mother is not well.'

A frozen moment. 'What kind of not well?'

Fabien shrugged, and made to take her in his arms.

But Briony swung in her tracks and hurried back to the campsite and the phone booth near the office. As she strode along she searched through her bag for a phone card, refusing with thanks Fabien's offer to make use of his parents' home, and the phone there.

Then she had a frustrating wait of ten minutes while a British family finished a lengthy call, but finally she was standing under the little canopy, dialling. And then, after a series of clicks and mini silences, suddenly she was listening to the measured, deep tones of her father.

'Dad? What's happened to Mum?'

After four days, Sarah was allowed home. Ellie flung herself on her, Guy holding onto Ripple's collar to prevent him from following suit. *'Mum! We've made a welcome home lunch! Chicken and salad and chocolate brownies!'* Ellie's brown eyes shone and her hair flew as she danced with delight.

Sarah hugged her daughter as if she'd been away for a month. 'All my favourite things!'

It was lovely to sit down as a family again in the bright dining room, circulating news with the bread-and-butter. Jim passed on phone messages to Guy, Dinah told Sarah proudly how Ellie had prepared the lunch with the minimum of supervision.

'And it's been delicious,' Sarah declared, setting down her knife and fork. 'Just what the doctor ordered, Ellie darling.' She wished her daughter's eyes would lose their expression of apprehension. But she was well aware that Ellie had been affected by her mother's sudden absence and was probably frightened of her disappearing again.

Guy reached for her empty plate and stacked it with his. 'Of course, what the doctor *actually* ordered was plenty of rest with some gentle exercise. And no stress.'

Sarah sniffed, pulling a face to make Ellie smile. 'That doesn't sound very exciting. And how on earth anyone achieves a life without stress is beyond me! I should think it's impossible.' She looked up with a broad grin, only to find Guy's dark eyes fixed on her severely.

'We're going to get you as near a stress-free life as *is* possible,' he promised, grimly. 'And we'd better get you stocked up with books and magazines, because a good read is about as strenuous as it's going to get for you for a while. You can certainly kiss goodbye to the office and that computer driving you up the wall.'

'So who…?' began Jim.

Sarah felt her eyes burn at Guy's stout intentions on her behalf. 'That would be lovely, darling, but *somebody* has to do it.'

He raised his eyebrows. 'But *not* you.' And, to his father, '*Not* Sarah – Ellie, would you mind answering the door, please? Ripple, calm down, you've heard the doorbell before! – because, sorry, Dad, but the doctor's had a stern word with me, and the office work's not Sarah's thing, and is too stressful for her. I blame myself for not replacing Pauline with someone properly trained in the first place. I don't want Sarah back in hospital until the baby's ready to make an appearance.'

Sarah heaved a longing sigh, her gaze flickering between her husband and her father-in-law. 'It would be lovely,' she confessed apologetically, 'but I just don't see how...'

Ellie interrupted her with a theatrical clearing of the throat. 'Ahem! Everybody, we have a guest!'

And Sarah turned with the others to see not one, but two daughters standing in the doorway. One a slight, sun-tanned figure with dark eyes and dark curly hair, two scuffed red suitcases beside her and a tatty backpack tall on her back.

'Briony!' Sarah gasped. After a moment when she was almost too stunned to react, she levered herself to her feet and raced around the table, joyful tears streaming down her face. 'Oh, Briony! Darling. You're here!'

She felt her daughter's strong young arms embrace her fiercely, even as the well-loved voice grumbled, 'But I thought you were supposed to be resting. If I'd known you were going to race round the room like Ellie's demented dog at the sight of me, I might've stayed in France!' But Sarah felt the arms tighten around her as her daughter added in a muffled voice, 'But it's *so good* to see you, again!'

Guy beamed as he hugged both daughter and wife in turn. 'Not as good as it is for us to see you. But what's this about living in a tent?'

Brought up short, Sarah glanced from one to the other. 'Yes, what *is* this about living in a tent?'

Guy and Briony exchanged guilty glances. 'Nothing!' Briony decided.

And Guy began scolding. 'What are you doing out of your seat, Sarah? You're supposed to be resting!'

After three weeks, the midwife declared Sarah's blood pressure to be much improved, and everyone could see that the swelling to her hands and feet was subsiding – although the same couldn't be said for her waistline! If she continued to be very sensible, it was expected that both she and the baby would make it safely to the fortieth weeks of her pregnancy.

It was safe, Guy decided, to call a family conference around the large polished dining table.

Dinah, Sarah and Briony were composed. Briony had come back to the family with a certainty of manner that proved how much she'd grown up. And she'd been a treasure in the past weeks, spending long hours before the dreaded pale grey computer to try and prevent the paperwork getting too badly out of hand. He'd almost forgiven her for not telling him about the tent.

Ellie looked alarmed, and Jim's chin jutted, as if to each the calling of a family meeting signified a conflict.

Guy began carefully. 'As we all know, everything changed for us last May. Briony went to France, we came home from Germany, a decision more-or-less forced upon us. Dad's angina got to the stage where he could no longer run the business.'

'That's what the doctors said,' Jim snorted, presumably forgetting his earlier exhaustion now he'd had several months of taking things easy.

'And it was uncomfortable for us,' Guy continued quietly, refusing to be drawn into an unnecessary debate. 'We had to react quickly to what life flung at us and, largely, put up with the way things happened. I was very concerned that Ellie, particularly, came out of it storm-tossed.'

Ellie gave him one of her quick, bright smiles, but she fidgeted uneasily with her brown hair, as if sensing something on the wind.

Guy looked around the table. 'Now there's another change in the offing. And this time I'm determined that every member of the family should get a chance to put their views.'

He went on to outline the offer from *O'Donahue Plant & Contracting*. 'I've already told Dad that I don't feel comfortable running *J R Randle*.' He smiled apologetically at his father, who nodded, but didn't smile. 'And also that I doubt, if *O'Donahue's* is to expand, that the business will remain profitable. We never formalised me taking over the business from him, so only he can make the decision whether to sell. But if he does sell, the bungalow will go with the business...'

He talked and talked, as if giving a presentation to the management of his old company, *G B Schwarz*, although nothing there had ever been as important as this, the happiness of his family. He talked about rising property prices and devaluing investments, about affording a home that would accommodate the growing family plus one pony-sized dog, about new jobs and new schools. About Briony's need to plan her next step, Ellie's need for security and a happy environment, about Jim and Dinah's health in their retirement. That the finding of a decent job would likely necessitate a move to another locality.

When he ran down, nobody spoke. He turned to Sarah. 'We've already discussed this, of course, but is there anything you want to add?'

Taking his hand, she smiled. 'I want you to be happy. That's as important as anything you've mentioned. With the new baby, I'm not going to be working outside the home for a while, so I can go wherever you go.'

He turned to his eldest daughter. 'Have you made any plans, Briony?'

She smiled, dreamily. 'I'd really like to go back to France.'

Guy felt his heart sink.

'Not back to Fabien!' she corrected, with a small grimace. 'I'm thinking more about Central France. But I'm not sure whether to make myself get some qualifications, first, or take low-paid and casual jobs, as I did before. I haven't decided yet.'

He looked at Ellie, who was stroking Ripple's head on her lap, and Ripple's black eyes glazing in an expression of bliss. 'Ellie? How do you feel about the possibility of changing school again?'

She sighed. 'I think I could cope better, now. I'd know more what to expect. I'd be sorry to leave Natalie, of course, but she has got other friends here.' When she looked up, her eyes were wet. 'But please let me keep Ripple!'

Any ideas Guy might have had to the contrary flew straight through the window open to the garden. 'Ripple's part of the family,' he said, firmly, sliding a comforting arm around her shoulders. 'Where we go, he goes.'

Lastly he turned to his parents. Dinah simply looked, in turn, at Jim.

'I've built this place up from nothing,' he declared, with a catch in his voice. 'I thought when you agreed to come into the business that it would carry on. Carry on after I'm gone.' He cleared his throat. 'But I've no right to expect that, really. I probably wasn't very understanding, boy.'

Guy found himself suddenly grinning. Only his father ever called him 'boy'.

Jim smoothed back his hair resignedly. 'Everyone's got to retire sometime. This seems like a good opportunity for your mother and me. I'd better ring O'Donahue and tell him I'm willing to listen to his offer.'

'You're good at putting yourself last, but we think it's important for you to be happy, too,' agreed Dinah.

Filled with relief, Guy sank back in his chair. 'Well. It seems that we're cautiously agreed that we're going. Now it's just a matter of deciding where we can afford property.'

A silence. Everyone looked at one another.

'*France!*' declared Briony, suddenly, eyes sparkling. 'Why don't we *all* go to France? Central France is comparatively cheap, I'll bet we could afford somewhere with enough room for the new baby and Ripple. Perhaps we could manage to buy a business? How about a nursery? I'd love to work with children.'

Guy stared at his eldest daughter. 'Actually, Briony, that *is* an idea worth investigating. There are programmes on the TV about the advantages of relocating in France, plenty of people seem to be taking the plunge.'

Sarah threw a doubtful look at Ellie. 'That throws up a problem with schools.'

Ellie got up suddenly from the table and rushed from the room, leaving an uncomfortable atmosphere in her wake.

'Maybe not,' Briony mumbled. 'Sorry if I've upset Ell, Mum. Bad enough for her beginning another school, but awful to be put in a French school when all she speaks is English and German. I don't suppose we could afford Germany?'

'It's more expensive than Britain.' Guy shook his head.

It was much later in the evening that Ellie returned to the rest of the family. After leaving the family meeting so precipitately, she'd shut herself away in the office with the computer. Tactfully, the family had assumed she needed a little time to herself, perhaps to e-mail her old friends in Germany. The meeting had broken up in her absence, and the family were relaxing with magazines or the television.

Guy looked up. Instead of Ellie wearing the sad or sulky expression at the prospect of more upheaval, which he'd anticipated, her expression was cautiously optimistic. 'There are international schools in places like Lyon, I've been looking it up on the Internet. And I've found out how you get to know about property for sale. And there are whole sites about moving to France. Even about pet passports, and everything.'

The family gaped at her. Guy found his voice first. 'So you wouldn't mind living there? If we could afford an international school?'

'I don't *th-i-nk* so,' said Ellie cautiously. 'At least it's worth investigating.'

'Definitely!' breathed Briony, eyes bright.

'Seems a good idea,' said Sarah, carefully, as if wary of getting her hopes up. She turned to her parents-in-law. 'I don't suppose you'd be interested in coming with us?'

Jim lay down his paper and cleared his throat. 'To be truthful, I was just thinking we could buy a good place, if we pooled our resources. And it would leave you more towards the school fees.' He winked at Dinah. 'Do you fancy another jaunt to France? You've still got half-shares in that dog, haven't you?'

Spacious 'people carriers' had replaced the old family cars, and they were just about fully packed, now. Briony shut the tailgate of her grandparents' sensible grey vehicle. Tomorrow, Guy would drive Jim, Dinah and herself in it on the first leg of the trip, while Sarah piloted the other – bright red –

vehicle containing Ellie, Ripple, and baby Alexander.

She smiled at the thought of her younger brother. Alex, already four months old, was adorable, a plump, beaming baby who was growing up with the idea that he had the benefit of at least four mothers – Sarah, Dinah, Briony and Ellie.

She opened the rear car door to check that Alex's car seat was firmly secured. Ellie would sit beside him, while Ripple napped on the floor. Ellie's lilac-coloured personal stereo was already on the seat. A sharp reminder of the days when they'd all lived in Germany. *'Schwarz muss nicht schwarz sein...'* ran through her head, the once-familiar marketing slogan of Guy's employer, *G B Schwarz*. 'Black doesn't have to be black'.

Her own shell-pink version was safely stowed in the other vehicle. Her favourite music would play through it to beguile the long journey of the next day.

They'd be over the channel by tomorrow afternoon, ready to find their hotel and stop for a couple of days in Normandy, making a holiday out of the journey to their new life.

She felt her heart swell at the thought of living in France again. She'd be able to meet up with Nicole and her other friends in Le

Puy, and perhaps even visit Uncle Ferdinand and Aunt Rose on their fermette, admire the rows of green vegetables and the fruit on the trees.

The legalities and formalities of the sale of the business to O'Donahue and the purchase of the new property had taken an excruciating length of time, but she'd spent it profitably, doing a part-time job as a nursery assistant and taking French lessons, and helping the rest of the family improve their grip on the language. Ellie was displaying her progress in the language by referring to Ripple *le grand chien idiot* – the big silly dog.

It had been great to have a spell in England and she was sure she'd live again amongst its rolling green fields sometime, but she enjoyed thinking of herself as a European. Or even a World Citizen. In fact, it was fast becoming her ambition to visit every country on the planet and learn of their colourful cultures and diverse people.

Everywhere was just so interesting.

She made sure she'd locked both vehicles, and turned away to spend her final night in her grandparents' bungalow.

'Briony?'

It was scarcely more than a whisper, but

she swung towards the sound, heart in her throat.

He stepped from the inky shadow by the gate, a huge rucksack strapped to his back. His hair was shorter than he'd worn it last summer.

She swallowed, her heart rushing. 'Fab! What on earth...?'

Slowly, he crossed the tarmac, stooped and brushed a kiss on each of her cheeks, his hands light and warm upon her shoulders. Then straightened. 'I walk, this Easter holiday. I walk in England. I think...' He looked around the yard, at the bungalow, back to her. 'I think, *peut-être*, that Briony might be pleased to see me. For old times.'

Suddenly, she had a painful lump in her throat. Once she'd been pleased to see Fab at any hour of the day. She wished her feelings were still so clear-cut. She swallowed with difficulty, and tried to make her voice light. 'You're lucky you found me. We leave tomorrow.'

'*Leave?*'

She laughed, shakily. 'For France! My grandparents and my parents have purchased property near Lyon, a big house with a flat, and three small cottages. Dad's bought a business franchise, too, he and his friend do you remember Josef, from Mikhlut? – are going to supply educational institutions with audio-visual equipment. Their office will be in the house, initially. We're going to let the cottages out to holidaymakers, Granddad fancies his hand at being in charge of that, if Gran will let him.'

'France,' he repeated, as if dazed. 'And I am in England.'

The spring evenings were only just lengthening, and it was already dark in the yard. Briony shivered, perhaps with the cold, or maybe at something in Fabien's voice. 'Would you like to come inside? Perhaps for a drink?'

He blinked. 'Thank you, but I come...' He hesitated. 'I come to tell to you some things. For you alone.'

His fingers groped for hers in the darkness, and she shivered at his touch.

And then, his words low and rapid, as if often rehearsed, he began, 'Briony, I receive my papers for the *armée*. At the end of this year I go to be an army doctor. I would like...' He paused again, as if trying to gauge her reaction. 'I would like very much to be again friends with you. I would like that we exchange letters.'

She drew in her breath.

216

He moved still closer, so that she could see the gleam of his smile, the shadow of his hair hanging above his eyes. 'And now you tell me you go to live in France.' He hesitated. 'Perhaps, in summer, your family has a little work for a man who likes to be in the country, to spend the *vacances* making work with his hands. You might be pleased if an old friend is the man.'

He lifted her hand to his mouth, and kissed her fingertips, a familiar caress. His voice became husky. 'Perhaps one day you forgive the man for pretending to be something he is not, for trying not to grow up.'

Her hands were growing warm in his. 'I don't know,' she admitted, hoarsely. 'I'll write to you, Fab, if that's what you want. But I don't know what'll happen. I might not even be living with my family next time you decide to work a season in your holidays. I might travel. I might walk through every country in the world. I might learn to climb mountains or help children in poor countries. Whatever I do, it'll be my decision.' Inside her chest was a fluttering, but she'd learnt, where Fab was concerned, to think with her head and not her heart.

There was a long, still moment before he stirred. '*Oui.* You can do anything Briony

Randle, you are strong. But still,' he pressed a little card into her hand. 'Still I give to you my address in Paris. And ask you to send to me your address near Lyon. Soon. I wait your letter. I am adult now. I no longer give up.'

He brushed a last salute to the back of her hand, then turned and melted into the darkness.

Hand tingling where his lips had been, she stood and listened to his footsteps echoing down the road. Straining to hear long after he'd gone.

The morning was clear with a suggestion of late frost in the air. The blossoming trees were like springtime brides, the fields green with spring's new growth, the sky high and blue.

Today the yard passed from *J R Randle* to *O'Donahue Plant & Contracting*. Today they would leave. Sarah glanced over at the bungalow where Jim and Dinah were turning the key in the front door for the last time. The petunia pots had gone now, the windows were blank without curtains.

Guy stirred beside her. 'It's a big moment for them.' His arm slid around her shoulder.

She leant against his warmth. Baby Alexander gurgled in his car seat. Ripple snuffled around the wheels of the car, his breath a white cloud in the chilly air.

Ellie and Briony came to stand beside their parents.

'Are Gran and Granddad sad? I thought they wanted to come and live in France with us?' Ellie petted Ripple's hairy ears, frowning.

'I'm sure their feelings are mixed. You've got to understand that this has been their work and their home for decades. You don't just rush away from that without a moment's thought.' Sarah watched as her parents-in-law embraced, Jim talking earnestly, Dinah dabbing at her eyes.

Yes, it was a huge change for Guy's parents, a huge change for them all. But, oh it was going to be a change for the better! Her heart soared. She thought of their new house, a spacious, gracious stone dwelling with a garden like a football field, room for even a carthorse like Ripple to bound about. For Ellie a trilingual school a bus ride away, for Guy a job where he wouldn't feel a fish out of water. And Josef and Marika living nearby again!

She put her hand on Briony's shoulder.

More importantly, they had their eldest

daughter with them, at least for a time. Till Briony's obvious restlessness took her away again to conquer new places. Sarah understood better now that Briony had her own stars to follow. This move to France, a long-term project for the rest of them, for her was only a beginning.

She wondered what would come next.

Briony had shown herself to be a deep, complex, determined young woman, who didn't share her innermost feelings until she was good and ready. Sarah sighed. She'd love to ask Briony why she'd become quiet and preoccupied yesterday evening, a mood that seemed to have stayed with her until morning. But she was a young woman, and Sarah would have to learn to respect her right to her own thoughts.

Ellie, she was almost sure, would grow up into a less complicated person, one whose face mirrored her emotions, compassions and joys. And Alex? Although he was already a little character, a noisy, chuckling, despot, it would be a while before they'd see what he'd make of life.

She slipped her arms around Guy's waist.

'Here they come,' he said. And a hush fell on the little group as Jim and Dinah descended the steps for the last time, arms linked, and made their way across the grey tarmac of the yard.

Jim looked down into his wife's eyes. 'Are you ready?'

Dinah nodded wordlessly.

Jim clapped his hand on his son's shoulder. 'Right then, boy. Shall we go? We've said our goodbyes now, put the past behind us. We're ready to jaunter off for a while. We're looking forward to the future.'

'Me, too,' agreed Sarah softly, taking out her car keys and clicking her fingers for Ripple to jump into the car. 'By this afternoon, we'll be in another country.'

This Large Print Book, for people
who cannot read normal print,
is published under the auspices of

THE ULVERSCROFT FOUNDATION

... we hope you have enjoyed this book.
Please think for a moment about those
who have worse eyesight than you ...
and are unable to even read or enjoy
Large Print without great difficulty.

You can help them by sending a
donation, large or small, to:

**The Ulverscroft Foundation,
1, The Green, Bradgate Road,
Anstey, Leicestershire, LE7 7FU,
England.**
or request a copy of our brochure for
more details.

The Foundation will use all donations
to assist those people who are visually
impaired and need special attention
with medical research, diagnosis
and treatment.

Thank you very much for your help.